unfinished

unfinished

a novel

by William C. Gordon

Bay Tree Publishing, LLC
Point Richmond, California

Calligraphy by Ward Schumaker
Cover design by Lori Barra and Sarah Kessler
Interior design by mltrees

Library of Congress Cataloging-in-Publication Data

Names: Gordon, William C. (William Charles), 1937-
Title: Unfinished : a novel / William C. Gordon.
Description: First edition. | Point Richmond, California : Bay Tree Publishing, LLC, [2015]
Identifiers: LCCN 2015037929 | ISBN 9780985939991 (softcover : acid-free paper)
Subjects: | GSAFD: Noir fiction.
Classification: LCC PS3607.O5947 U54 2015 | DDC 813/.6--dc23
LC record available at http://lccn.loc.gov/2015037929

This book is dedicated to

Michele Batany and Ana Cejas

Table of Contents

Part 1

1

Looking for Clues

SAMUEL HAD BEEN ON an extended vacation when two boys were murdered within six weeks of each other in the same alleyway South of Market. They both attended the exclusive, private Towne School.

A crime reporter for the afternoon paper, Samuel made his name by solving the murder of a friend and drinking buddy in Chinatown. Since then he had helped Lieutenant Bruno Bernardi, head of the San Francisco Police Department homicide squad, identify the perpetrators in several high profile murder cases. His articles about these cases made the front page.

After talking about the two murder cases with Bernardi he went to the evidence room and handed the wrinkled clerk a note from Bernardi that allowed him access.

"You again, Hamilton," the small man said as he smiled. "Can I give you a suggestion?"

"Sure, what is it?"

"If I were you, I'd go over and talk to the medical examiner first, since his people are the ones who gathered the evidence."

"Not a bad idea. I'll have to track him down. See you in a few." Samuel wandered next door to the medical examiner's office and made arrangements to talk with him.

The clerk went down the hall to confirm that the message

came from Bernardi.

Within a short time, Barney McLeod came walking slowly towards them, and when he saw Samuel, he said, "What can I help you with, Mr. Bloodhound?"

"It's about those two kidnap victims who were murdered."

"He put you on these two, did he?" A pathologist by training, the medical examiner had been at the job for many years and had a national reputation for his astute forensic abilities. Tall and angular, he was affectionately called Turtle Face because of his melancholy look and the fact that his head was stuck out of his body the way a turtle's head sticks out of its shell.

"Yeah. Someone has to do the dirty work. Now that you're here, Barney, can we have a chat about these cases?"

"Sure, come back to my office." McLeod turned and walked back down the hall with Samuel following him. He sat down hard behind his neatly organized desk. In one corner presided a real skeleton. Behind him was a rogue's gallery of photos on the wall. There were several files stacked on the right side of his desk, and one was open on the ink blotter directly in front of him.

"Can you give me a rundown on what you think happened in these two cases?"

"Sure," said Turtle Face. "The boys were killed six weeks apart with the same gun, a .38. If we find the gun, we find the killer. From the looks of it, the same person, probably a man, wrote two incoherent ransom notes that weren't really ransom notes because he apparently intended to kill both boys from the moment he abducted them."

"Why do you say that?"

"Because he didn't give anybody time to react. The notes came out the day each boy was kidnapped, and the next day the boy was found dead South of Market in the same alleyway. Both boys went to the Towne School up in Pacific Heights.

Imagine what that's done to foster public interest in these cases. The rich kids got it."

"Any fingerprints or other physical clues that you know of?"

"We think that the same gun was used in both deaths, but we only have one bullet. The other one passed through the boy's head and wasn't found at the scene. Either it lodged somewhere in the alley where he was killed or it disintegrated on impact."

"Did your people look for it?" asked Samuel.

"Yeah, but no dice. I told Bernardi about it, so maybe he followed up on it."

"This is the first I've heard of it, so I doubt it."

"The fact that we have a bullet at all shows that the killer made a mistake," said Turtle Face.

"What do you mean?"

"From the looks of the crime scene, this guy knew what he was doing, and leaving a bullet that could eventually be traced to a gun was a no-no."

"Some good news, anyway. You said it was a .38. Is that a common hand gun?"

"Sure is. More powerful than a .22 and not as lethal as a .45, but in trained hands, deadly. The police use .45s. And we can't honestly tell if whoever used this weapon against those boys was a gun expert. Some say that because only one bullet lodged in one of their bodies, he wasn't such a sharp cookie. But maybe he wanted everyone to know that he was using a .38, and that he meant business."

"In other words, arrogance or stupidity," said Samuel.

"I think it was arrogance. As I said, this didn't look like a mistake. In my opinion, you're dealing with someone who knew exactly what he was doing."

"Is there anything else you remember as being significant?"

"To tell you the truth, I thought that they were both too clean. He only left clues that he wanted the police to find and that couldn't be traced back to him."

"What about the .38 slug?"

"Do you know how many .38s there are in this state? Thousands, so it will be almost impossible to find the exact weapon. You can bet it wasn't a registered gun anyway, and no doubt it's long gone by now. So no one is going to bother looking into who has a license to carry one in this state. If the murderer gets arrested for something else and just happens to still have the weapon, that's another thing. But you should take another look at the evidence. We might have overlooked something. Why not take Bernardi's tech with you? He's good at that stuff. If we didn't miss anything, we may never find out who did them in."

"That's why I'm here. The clerk told me to come over and talk to you before I take a look at the evidence over at homicide. I hope my extra pair of eyes will serve that purpose. If I find anything, I'll get Phillip McIntosh right on it. He's Bernardi's forensic tech."

Samuel got up and went back to the homicide evidence locker. "I'm ready to go over what you've got," he told the clerk. "Do you want to sit in with me?"

"You know I have to; besides, I'd like to be a witness when you find the clue, or clues, that solve these cases." He dug into the back of the locker where the shelves were stacked with evidence boxes for cases that were open for investigation. He pulled out two, each with a different name on it.

Samuel carried one while the clerk took the other down the hall to a conference room where they spread the contents of each box on a separate table. They somberly looked at the socks, pants, soiled underwear, blood spattered shirts and jackets. The clothes were similar, preppy-styles for boys from well-heeled families. Samuel put his notebook on the table and painstakingly examined each article of clothing and found nothing. Then he took a magnifying glass out of his coat pocket and repeated the process. He finally zeroed in on the collar of the first murdered boy's jacket.

"Take a look at this. Is that a very small feather?" he asked the clerk.

The small man came over and looked through the magnifying glass. "Sure looks like it," he said.

Samuel looked at the other boy's clothing in the same place. "I'll be damned," he said. There was more than one on each of the collars of their jackets and even on their shirts. "Can you tell what kind of feather this is?"

"Don't have a clue," said the clerk.

"What's that black streak on the pant leg of those expensive khakis?"

"It's not mentioned in the report."

"Can I borrow your phone? I think it's time to get Mac down here."

Samuel called Mac, and he came down to the room where the evidence was spread out. They both went over it for more than an hour taking copious notes. As they were finishing, Samuel pointed to a speck of something dull embedded in one of the collars. Mac took the clerk's magnifying glass and motioned to Samuel to have a look. They both concluded that it was a small piece of lead.

"I think it's a part of a bullet, probably the one they couldn't find at the scene," he said after he reviewed the notes of the medical examiner's investigator. "Looks like you and I should get out there and take another look, Samuel."

2

Who Would Steal a Child?

THE FADED YELLOW VOLKSWAGEN bus drove slowly down Twenty-fifth Street and maneuvered into the empty parking space, a couple of blocks from James Lick School. The driver got out and removed the sawhorse with the white cardboard sign marked RESERVED in bold black letters. He lifted the rear hatch of the bus, thrust the sign and sawhorse into the baggage compartment, and shut it. Then he went around to the curb, slid open the panel door, and got in the empty space where the middle seat had been. He closed the door, reached into the front to turn on a classical music station, sat back and waited.

It was just before three in the afternoon, a warm day in the late winter of 1964. He heard the school bell ring as the students began spilling out like marbles from the pumpkin-colored stucco school building. One of them was Alain Sheridan, a tall eleven-year-old with dark brown hair and blue eyes who was carrying several books under his arm. As he skipped down the sidewalk, he tried to avoid stepping on the lines in the cement. He was on his way home to the house on Twenty-fifth Street just beyond Church where he lived with his mother, Emma, and his grandmother, Reyna. It was Friday, and he was happily thinking of the fun he and his friend Jacob would have the next day. They were going on a long afternoon outing to the zoo, and then for a pizza dinner on Twenty-fourth Street with their combined allowances.

As Alain approached the Volkswagen bus, the driver got up and reached over the front seat and turned off the radio. He then made sure the children walking ahead of Alain were not looking in his direction. Any indication that they were, and his mission would have to be aborted. He moved closer on the seat to the curbside and dowsed a terrycloth hand towel in chloroform. When Alain was two sidewalk squares away, the man opened the door and grabbed him, placing the towel over the boy's mouth and nose. Alain initially struggled and tried to cry out, but the chloroform overcame him, and he collapsed limply into the arms of his abductor.

He dragged the boy into the open back door of the bus, gathered up his books from the sidewalk, slid the door closed behind him, and laid him down on the floor. The man placed tape over his mouth, bound his wrists behind his back, and tied his ankles. He used more tape to secure the body to the underside of the front seat, so the child wouldn't roll around. Since less than two minutes had elapsed, he stopped worrying about the children who'd rushed ahead of Alain. None of them had turned to see what might have happened. He did see one person turn the corner and walk towards the bus, but he seemed too far away to pose a threat.

* * *

Emma Sheridan was sitting on her back porch eyeing her latest canvas. A petite woman with blond hair she wore in a ponytail, she had a calm appearance, deep blue eyes, and a sensitive mouth. She looked every bit the talented artist she was. Staring out at her garden, she got up and stretched. Aided by a cane, she backed up a few feet, squeezing easily between the end table and the couch to look at her work.

At that moment Reyna Henri walked into the room with a pot of tea and two cups. Reyna was a dark-haired Algerian woman with strong straight black hair and an aquiline nose. She was Emma's and Alain's adopted mother and grandmother respectively. Emma had brought Reyna from France when she and Alain came to the United States after the woman's daughter had died. She had been married to a French general who was assassinated by the rebels during the Algerian uprising.

Emma asked Reyna, "Is the yellow too strong? Have I overstated the importance of the lavender in the painting? Is the dab of red splashed on the right side of the canvas enough to bring the observer's eye over there?"

"Honestly Emma, you keep painting the same landscape over and over again. What's with you? Would you like me to add a few strokes or just give my opinion?" she smiled.

"It is a very nostalgic place for me. It is where Ian and I conceived our son. Now that he is gone, I want to recreate it for my own peace of mind." She glanced at the clock, which showed that it was after four.

"It seems odd that Alain is not home from school yet, since it is only blocks away," said Reyna. "I took the macaroni and cheese that I had prepared for him as a snack out of the oven and put it on the kitchen counter. Did he say he would be late?"

"We'll give him a few more minutes," said Emma, still looking absentmindedly at the painting.

When he had still failed to return at 4:30, Emma called the school and found out that Alain was not there. Butterflies fluttered in her stomach as she grabbed her cane and hobbled to the door. She asked Reyna to wait there in case Alain showed up so that he wouldn't come home to an empty house. She went down the stairs of their house to the street and walked as quickly as she could the two blocks to the school. She went directly to the principal's office where she saw the woman sitting behind her desk going over a pile of papers.

"Excuse me, Mrs. Snodgrass," she said in a quavering voice with a French accent. "My son Alain did not come home from school. When I called, they said he wasn't here. Can you help me?"

"Of course, dear," said the stern-looking older woman. With a pained look on her face, she asked, "When did you call?"

"It was only a few minutes ago. I rushed up here from my home two blocks away." She wiped beads of perspiration from her forehead.

"Oh Lord, you live that close, and it's been over two hours?" The expression on the woman's faced turned from pain to fear. The corners of her mouth arched downward.

"Do you think we should call the police?" said Emma.

"Maybe we should wait," she suggested—no doubt worrying about unnecessarily generating negative publicity. "Are you sure he didn't have something to do or somewhere to go? Maybe he forgot to tell you. Does he have a girlfriend?"

"At his age, he's into comic books and TV reruns of Howdy Doody and Hopalong Cassidy," said Emma, "not girls."

Mrs. Snodgrass now seemed truly nervous. Emma could see that the flowered dress she was wearing had moistened under the armpits. She picked up the telephone with a tremulous hand and dialed the number of the precinct captain. When he answered the phone, she introduced herself and explained the situation. She listened in silence for several seconds then hung up, telling Mrs. Sheridan that the officer would be there shortly, and asking if she would like a cup of tea.

"No, thank you, I'll just sit over here and wait." Emma moved toward one of the chairs in the principal's office and sat down.

19

Within minutes two policemen walked into Mrs. Snodgrass's office. The taller one introduced himself as Captain Markel from the San Francisco Police Department. He had a strong jaw and brown eyes widely separated. When he smiled, he revealed slightly stained yellow teeth. He introduced his shorter colleague as Sergeant McGregor. The sergeant was almost stout and had a food stain on the lapel of his uniform.

"We understand your boy didn't come home from school today, is that correct?" asked the captain.

"Yes, and that is not at all like him," she replied.

"He is a very conscientious boy, very standoffish with the other children but also brilliant," pitched in Mrs. Snodgrass.

"Is it possible he went to a friend's house to spend the afternoon?"

"He would never do that without asking permission," said Emma. "We are alone in this country with only his grandmother. We have good communication between the three of us."

"Where are you from, ma'am?" asked the captain.

"Alain and I are both from France."

"How long have you been in the U.S.?"

"It has been about five years now."

"What do you do for a living?"

"I am an artist. A portrait painter, mostly by commission, so I am at home most of the time."

"Tell me about your son: his date of birth, what his habits are, what he likes to do in his spare time, and, of course, whether he has any special problems that might help us locate him."

"Alain was born in France eleven years ago. His father was an American who was recently killed in Vietnam. It was a terrible loss for him and for me too."

"Tell me about your son's daily activities."

"He is a very good student," interrupted Mrs. Snodgrass.

"He is what you call a homebody," his mother added. "He is very involved in his studies. He is on the sixth grade honor role, as he has been in all his grade levels."

"No outside interests that would take him to a different part of the city without telling you?

"No. If he had something special to do, he would have let me know, and I would have accompanied him," she said, beginning to be bothered by the barrage of questions. Why weren't they taking action instead?

"That's all for now, Mrs. Sheridan. We need a recent photograph. I can send the sergeant home with you so you can provide us with one."

"That won't be necessary," the principal interjected. "We can provide one from our file here at school, and we can give you a copy of his medical report, which was just completed."

3

Samuel's Painful Revisit to His Past

Samuel heard the report of Alain's kidnapping on the police band of his radio and began trembling with anxiety. How could something like this happen? Emma Sheridan was an unusual enough name that he knew this had to be the woman he had badly injured while he was drunk several years before. His reckless behavior, along with the brutal murder of his parents shortly before that, had contributed to his descent into drunkenness and deep depression. Fortunately, his huge insurance policy had paid her a very large settlement. He had narrowly avoided going to jail because of the skill of a young San Francisco attorney but had lost his driver's license for three years as a result of the accident.

After wallowing in self-pity and profound shame for more than a year after the accident, he started to emerge from the depths of his despair and self-loathing. The first step on his road to recovery, which eventually earned him a job as a reporter, was to get a position at the morning paper selling ads on a commission basis. The pay was so meager that he could barely cover his tab at Camelot, a Nob Hill bar where he regularly ate dinner at the hors d'oeuvre table. He was fortunate to make friends with Melba, the owner, who turned out to be a valuable connection as well.

He visited Emma in the hospital every day after the accident to apologize for his actions and to assure her that he would do all he could to make up for it. Then he forced his insurance company to pay her medical bills and to offer her a substantial settlement. At first, she'd been furious with him, but in time she realized the damage was done, and she would have to get used to her altered physical condition.

Once he was earning a salary, Samuel began to help her financially. It wasn't just guilt that propelled him. She was a very talented artist, and he wanted her to succeed and overcome the injury he caused. Finally, she had said that she forgave him, which brought some relief to his damaged conscience.

He'd recently started talking with Blanche, his girlfriend, about Emma, and had invited his girlfriend to go with him to meet her.

But now this terrible thing had happened.

It was after eight at night when he phoned Emma, who answered immediately, and he told her that he'd just heard the awful news about her son.

Emma burst into tears. "Samuel, I'm so worried. Can you please come to my house?"

"I'll be there as fast as a cab can get me there," he answered.

He put on his wrinkled sports coat, rushed from his office on Market Street, hailed a cab, and was at her front door within twenty minutes.

When she opened the door, she again burst into tears as she embraced him. "This is the worst thing that has ever happened to me," she confessed.

"I know it's hard, Emma, but I'm here to help. I'll be by your side until we find him." Reyna was behind her and offered him a cup of tea.

Samuel didn't disclose all. Nothing could be worse than to have Alain go missing with the perpetrator of two child murders still at large. Still, he was pretty sure that she didn't follow the news and wouldn't know about the other two boys. On his way over to her house, he'd decided to drop everything else and concentrate all his energy on bringing Alain safely home. He wouldn't mention Bernardi's name or his own role in the homicide investigations because he didn't want to frighten her.

"Can you tell me what you know?" said Samuel.

"Just that he didn't come home from school. After four, I went over there and reported him missing."

"Can I see his room?"

She grabbed her cane and guided him to Alain's bedroom. They were followed by Reyna. It was a tidy refuge for the young boy. He had a poster of Rin Tin Tin on one wall, and of Elvis Presley and the Beatles on the other, and one of maritime knots on the third. Beneath it was a desk in perfect order. There was a bookcase containing five volumes of Gibbon's *The Decline and Fall of the Roman Empire* and next to it the complete works of Jules Verne and a dog-eared copy of *Robinson Crusoe.* Then, he spied *The Boy Scout Handbook,* and *The U. S. Army Manual for Survival in the Wilderness,* and several comic books along with novels by Agatha Christie. Lesser dime detective novels filled the rest of the shelves. In a separate bookcase, there were several volumes of *National Geographic* with articles on survival.

"Has he read all those books?" asked Samuel.

"Oh yes," answered Emma. "He's a good reader and he takes notes." She opened a drawer and showed Samuel a thick notebook where he'd written about each book or article in crisp legible handwriting. Each work that he studied was separated by a plastic sheet.

"Was he also reading that book on physics that's open on his desk?" asked Samuel.

"Yes, he is quite a whiz at mathematics and physics, even

though they don't teach physics in school until he is much older."

"Where did he get those aptitudes?"

"From his father and from my father. Mine was a pilot during the war and he had a very mathematical mind. In addition, he could build anything from what you Americans call 'scratch.' That's why Alain loved Robinson Crusoe so much. He said it reminded him of his grandfather."

"I remember your telling me about your father. And I knew that Alain's father was quite accomplished at physics. Didn't he end up as a patent lawyer here in San Francisco? He had an advanced degree in Mechanical Engineering."

"Yes, before he went to Vietnam he worked for a patent law firm for a couple of years."

"Your son's knowledge of physics and gadgetry may help him get home safely," said Samuel.

The muscles in Emma face tightened. "Do you know something that you're not telling me, Samuel?"

"No," Samuel lied. "Just thinking out loud. I'd like to return and read his notes on Agatha Christie's mysteries if you don't mind? You and Reyna come and sit with me in your living room, Emma. I've been meaning to come and see you for the last year and catch up. Let's talk."

They sat down on a sofa covered with a unique blue and red batik fabric. On the wall behind it hung one of Emma's landscapes with touches of the same colors.

"That painting looks like it's worth a lot of money," said Samuel, trying to change the subject.

"I was offered a lot for it, but I couldn't part with it. It had too much sentimental value. I painted it just when Ian and I got back together, when I was recuperating from my accident." She stopped talking, and he saw her swallow hard. "I'm sorry Samuel, I can't flit around to other things right now. All my thoughts and energy are on Alain."

"I understand that. When I leave here, I'm going to police headquarters to see if I can help with the investigation. I'll keep you up to date on everything I find out. In the meantime, if he's not back tonight, I'd like you to see a psychologist. My friend Ana Cejas lives right here in your neighborhood."

"What's that about, Samuel?"

"You've been through a lot; much more than just the injuries that I caused you. And I think you need to talk to someone. I'll pay for it."

"Who is this person?"

"A therapist. She can help you deal what's happening right now, plus some of the other things that I think are haunting you."

"It's very kind of you, Samuel, but as I said, right now, all I can think about is Alain."

"Okay. We'll talk tomorrow."

He left, trying to conceal his apprehension, but he knew she and Reyna both sensed it. He needed to get to Bernardi as soon as possible.

* * *

Samuel walked up to Castro, found a phone booth by the market at 24th Street and dialed Bernardi's home number. "I'm sure you know there's been another kidnapping," he began. "This time it's the son of a friend of mine. Can I come over?"

"Sure." Bernardi's voice sounded tired. "Should I put on a pot of coffee, or do you want something stronger?"

"This calls for coffee."

He hailed a cab and was at Bernardi's apartment within ten minutes.

"What do you know about this one?" asked Samuel.

"It's strange," Bernardi said. "Whoever did it took the kid

right off the street in broad daylight. According to the report, they've put out an all-points bulletin with a description of the boy. Other than that they haven't done anything, because most of the witnesses, if there are any, are the children who were walking home from school."

"Who's going to do the investigation?"

"It can't be me or my department because there's been no homicide yet, but I asked to be kept in the loop because of the other two cases that you and I are following."

"Why did you say yet?" said Samuel, worried. "Do you have any reason to think that it fits the pattern of the other two?"

Bernardi started pacing the floor. "The first act is always the same, an abductor snatches someone. After that, we have to wait to see what develops. In each of the recent fatal ones, there were unintelligible ransom notes. Before anyone could respond, each boy was found shot dead in the same alley South of Market. Obviously the kidnapper never intended to have a dialogue with anyone or release either of those boys. They were goners from the minute they were picked up.

"I have a call in to Sergeant Patruski. He's the one who's in charge of investigating these kidnappings unless they turn into homicides."

"Have you talked to him?" asked Samuel. "Obviously whoever grabbed them knew their routines."

"It's going to take some snooping to find out how he or she made that connection," said Bernardi.

"It's a man," said Samuel, as he stood up. "Your handwriting expert confirms that in his report. But there are some key differences with this new kidnapping. Alain is not the son of a Pacific Heights big shot, he's the child of an artist whose father was killed in Vietnam. There's no chance of a big ransom payoff."

"Someone may have seen the kidnapping," said Bernardi. "Call Patruski tomorrow. He'll be available around 8:00 A.M. I'll be there too."

27

* * *

Samuel was with Sergeant Ivan Patruski, going over the evidence file on Alain's kidnapping, when Bernardi arrived the next morning. The sergeant informed Samuel that he was heading to the school. "Mrs. Snodgrass has gathered the kids who walk to and from school along the same route as the kidnap victim. I'm going to take statements from them with her present."

"Can I come along?" asked Samuel.

"It's okay with me. What do you say, Lieutenant?" asked the tall thin man.

"Sure, Samuel helps us gather information. You know that from the other two kidnap cases."

"Just checking. Samuel's a good sleuth, I know that," said Patruski.

Samuel accompanied the sergeant to James Lick School where they met Captain Markel. In her office Mrs. Snodgrass greeted them with a taut face. Captain Markel introduced Sergeant Patruski and excused himself. After learning that there was a reporter present, Mrs. Snodgrass seemed even more anxious, but the sergeant reassured her that Samuel wouldn't say a word until the case was solved. "The children are very scared about this whole thing. I hope you won't question them too intently," said Mrs. Snodgrass.

"We're just trying to find out if they saw anything," said Patruski. "How many do you have for us to interview?"

"There were four children walking down the same street that Alain takes to go home. They're all outside, waiting to talk with you." She ushered in the four. "These boys were all ahead of him and they were in a group."

Samuel and Patruski looked them over. "What grade are you boys in?" asked the sergeant.

The tallest boy responded. "We're all in Alain's class, the

sixth grade. We were in a group ahead of him, and we didn't see anything unusual. He was behind us, and then he wasn't."

Both the sergeant and Samuel had taken down the boy's name. "At some point, you saw Alain, and then at some point, you didn't?"

"Yes, sir. We all knew he was behind us because he went to his locker to pick up some books."

"Can you tell us how many?" asked the sergeant.

"Can't say," said the boy. "A stack of them."

"And when you noticed that he wasn't behind you, did you hear anything?" asked Samuel.

The boy thought for a moment. "I heard tires screech, and that's when we turned around, and he wasn't there."

"Do you other boys agree with that, that that's what made you turn around?" asked the sergeant.

The other boys nodded.

"When you turned around, did you figure out what was making the screeching sounds?" asked Samuel.

"Yes, sir," the tall boy answered. "I saw a Volkswagen bus making a U-turn up the street."

"Was the bus between you and the school?" asked the sergeant.

"Yes, sir."

"Did you pass it when you were walking home from school?" asked Samuel.

"I think so, I'm not sure."

"What about any of the rest of you?" asked the sergeant.

Two of the boys nodded. One of them said, "I think it was parked at the curb."

"Was it parked on the same side of the street you were walking on?"

"Yes, sir," answered the boy.

"Did you see anybody in the bus?"

"I saw a man with a gray beard," the boy answered. "He

was listening to the radio."

"What kind of a beard?" asked Samuel.

"Short and sort of pointed," the boy said.

"Could you tell what kind of music he was listening to?" asked Samuel.

"Yes, sir. It was classical music, like the kind my mother likes."

"Do you know if the bus that made the U-turn was the same one that was earlier parked at the curb?" asked Samuel.

"I don't know."

The first boy who had spoken said, "The bus that made the U-turn was a dull yellow, I remember that."

"Can you show us where the bus was originally parked?" asked Samuel.

"I think so," answered the boy who had first identified the parked bus.

"How far away?" asked the sergeant.

"About a block up the street."

The sergeant looked to Mrs. Snodgrass. "Can we borrow your students for a few minutes?"

"Of course," she answered. "I'll come with you."

The group left the building and walked down the street. The boy pointed to the place where he thought it had first parked. A couple of other boys agreed. Samuel asked where the bus made the U-turn. The group walked another half block down the street. They all pointed to the same place. There were some tire tracks on the pavement. "We better get our people out here," said Patruski. "I can radio as soon as I get back to my car."

As they were walking back up the hill to the school, Samuel asked if any of them had noticed the bus hanging around before.

"I think so," said one of the boys. "I'm pretty sure I saw it parked near there before."

"Any of the rest of you see it?" he asked.

They all shook their heads in the negative.

"I think I have enough," said the sergeant. "Thank you, boys, and Mrs. Snodgrass. I'll have to come back in a few minutes and get each one of them to give a separate statement. Right now, I have to get to my car and radio to the station to get a photographer and some technical people out here to deal with those tire tracks."

He started to walk up the street to his patrol car as the boys and the principal went back to school.

"I'll stick around here for a few minutes until you get back, Sergeant."

"Suit yourself. I'll be right back."

After Patruski left, Samuel went to the place where the boy said the car had been parked. He started knocking on doors of houses that were closest to the place indicated by the boy. The first two were duds, but at the third house, he had some results. A middle-aged woman with an apron, gray hair, and glasses answered.

"Excuse me, ma'am. I'm from the afternoon paper, and I'm helping the police look for a missing student from the school. You may have heard about it on the radio today?"

"I did hear something on KCBS this morning," she said. "It's a terrible thing to happen to any family, and such a young child."

"Did you see a yellow Volkswagen bus parked out in front of your house yesterday?"

She thought for a moment. "Now that you mention it, I did see one. Around noon there was a white sign on a sawhorse with writing on it that said, No Parking or Reserved, or something like that. The next thing I knew, the sign was gone and there was this yellow Volkswagen bus parked there."

Samuel's head shot up. "Really? Do you know what time that was?"

She squinted. "I would say it was about two o'clock when I saw the bus, and a couple of hours before when I saw the sawhorse with the sign on it."

"Did you see anything else?"

"There was a man in the bus. He had gray hair and a very fashionable beard. I had to go to the doctor. When I left the house I walked right by him, never giving it another thought until you mentioned it."

"That's plenty," said Samuel. I need to take down your name and address if you don't mind?" He was beaming at this stroke of luck.

"Okay." She paused. "Oh, I remember one other thing. The passenger window was open because it was a warm day, and the man was listening to classical music."

"Did you notice if the bus had California plates?" he asked.

She thought. "No, that didn't register with me."

Samuel gave her his card. "Just in case you remember anything else. You can reach me at this number in the daytime, and I've written my home phone number on the back."

Samuel started walking up the street towards the school. By that time the sergeant had returned. He recounted what he'd learned, and they walked back down the street to wait for the evidence unit to arrive to measure the tire tracks. Samuel made inquiries at the houses on both sides of the street, but most people weren't home at that time of the day, and he didn't learn anything new.

* * *

In the early afternoon, Samuel walked into Bernardi's office at 850 Bryant Street, overlooking the eastbound lanes of the 101 Freeway as it merged with Highway 80 and approached the Bay Bridge. He repeated what he had learned at the school and in the neighborhood with the boys and told him about the woman that had given him a description of the driver.

"Can you believe our luck?"

"This might be our first break in all three cases," said Bernardi.

"I'm not ready put these three cases in the same pot," said Samuel. "This kid is from a different part of the city, and he's not of the same social class as the other two. Besides, with me, this one is personal. I know the boy and his mother."

"We can't sit on our hands, either," said Bernardi. "The same kidnapper definitely killed two kids, and another one is missing. We need to find this one fast, and hope that history doesn't repeat itself."

"The sergeant's checking with the Department of Motor Vehicles to find out how many yellow Volkswagen buses are registered in the State of California, and are located in Northern California," said Samuel.

"Let's hope at least one of them is registered right here in San Francisco," said Bernardi.

"The sergeant asked the woman to come down to the station and look at mug shots," said Samuel. "I'm going to sit in when she's going over them this afternoon."

"Okay. Keep me posted," said Bernardi. "What's your next move?"

"After the meeting, I need to find the owner of that bus, and make sure we at least match the owner's identity with the vehicle."

Bernardi looked worried, but Samuel was beside himself with agitation. He wanted to get results, now that he had something to go on.

* * *

33

That afternoon Samuel met with Sergeant Patruski and the woman who had seen the kidnapper, but they found nothing new. He went back to Bernardi's office where the DMV teletype results had come in. They went over the list of buses that were registered in San Francisco.

There was one that was listed as owned by Marcus Johns with an address near the beach in the Sunset District. Samuel asked Bernardi to drive him out to the address so they could check it out. It was powder blue and parked in front of the owner's house and had a sign on it that said Johns Summer Camp with a phone number. They rang the bell at the house and Bernardi introduced himself and talked to the owner, a college boy who ran a summer camp. He was tall, slim, well-groomed, and extremely well-spoken.

"Sorry," said Bernardi, "we were just checking for VW buses in San Francisco. We were looking for a yellow one, and that's not yours. Please excuse our inquiry."

"That's quite all right, Lieutenant. Hope you find who you're looking for," said Johns, and he closed the door.

4

The Getaway

THE BUS MADE A HURRIED U-turn before it reached the children who were ahead of Alain. As it did, the tires squealed. The crowd of children turned around in surprise, but it was too late to worry about them. He made his way back to Castro Street, turned right, and headed up the hill, watching children streaming into the markets to buy afternoon sugary treats.

He drove several blocks up Castro Street, parked the bus and crawled over the seat to inspect his cargo. He'd risked a lot to capture this treasure, and he wanted to make sure that he hadn't damaged it. He took out a stethoscope and listened to the child's heartbeat and his slow steady breathing. He smiled and took the tape off the boy's mouth because he knew that a side effect of the drug was nausea and vomiting.

Climbing back into the driver's seat, he turned on the classical music station that he'd been listening to before and lowered the volume so as not to wake his slumbering captive.

He had prepared a hiding place in the mountains of Big Sur but had to be careful not to break any traffic laws on the way. He drove for an hour south on the 101 and past San Jose where the freeway ended and the fruit orchards were just waking from their winter sleep. There were traces of foliage beginning to appear on their branches. He had to pull over when his captive started to vomit.

He went to the rear, opened the back, and took out some white terrycloth face towels plus two small buckets, one with water and the other empty. He changed the boy's position, so he wouldn't choke on his own vomit, and cleaned him and the area he was lying in. The boy, dazed and groggy, looked up at him with terror and confusion in his eyes. The abductor observed the boy's struggling and ignored his desperation. He started driving again.

After he'd passed Morgan Hill and was in sugar beet country, he pulled over and again checked his cargo. The boy was becoming restless. He ignored the pleading eyes and gave him another towel of chloroform. Again, he checked the boy's heart with his stethoscope and then continued his journey, turning right onto Highway 156. He passed the dunes of Sand City and Fort Ord where the humid sea air and fog from Monterey Bay drifted over the highway. He continued past Carmel Bay and the forest of Point Lobos and continued south on Highway 1 until he reached the outskirts of Big Sur. Once there, he turned onto a dirt road that took him up to an isolated goldmine claim high in the mountains overlooking the Pacific.

He pulled the VW bus into a parking space next to some wooden stairs. He quickly got out and peered into the side window, checking for the boy; he then walked down the stairs to the locked door of the lower cabin. He unlocked its three deadbolts and let himself inside. The padded room had only a small window some eight feet above the floor that allowed light to enter the room from the east. The room was bare, except for an army cot with three folded blankets on it at one end and a pillow on the other. There was a propane heater outlet in the ceiling. He could faintly hear the waves hitting the rocks far below with their constant rhythmical thuds.

Satisfied that everything was in order, he relaxed a little as he walked back up the stairs to the VW. He opened the sliding back door and bundled the child. He dragged the boy out of the bus, threw him over his shoulder, and went back down the stairs to the padded room. He put the unconscious boy on the cot and covered him with two blankets. Almost immediately, Alain started throwing up again. His captor unbound him, so he could position him in a way that would prevent the boy from choking on his own vomit. He then retrieved a stepladder from the storeroom next door and used it to reach and turn on the intercom he'd installed in the ceiling to monitor noises from his captive. He scribbled a note explaining that there was water and hot tea in the two thermoses. Then he left and locked the door.

Upstairs, he turned on the radio receiver. He could hear the boy retching, but since he was breathing, the man was not worried.

5

Ana Cejas

A PSYCHOTHERAPIST WHO had studied in Argentina, Ana Cejas was also certified to practice in California. But she was much more than just a psychotherapist, she was also a fine artist, an expert in aromatherapy, astrology, and many of the healing arts. Samuel knew her background when he arranged an appointment for Emma Sheridan. He wanted Emma to have an outlet to talk about Alain's disappearance two days before. The police investigation was going ahead, and Samuel could see the toll it was taking on Emma. He hoped she could start to come to terms with the many other losses in her life, including the horrible accident he'd caused. He assured her that he would be working overtime, following all the leads that could possibly help find her son.

Together Samuel and Emma walked the couple of blocks to Ana's two-story home where she had her office. Emma was exhausted. She had not slept in days and was sick with worry.

They approached the wrought iron gate and rang the bell. On it were two overlapping circles.

"I know that symbol, said Emma, her voice cracking, "it's the *vesica piscis.*"

He released the latch and the gate opened. "What does that mean?" he asked.

"You want the translation from Latin? I would say that

'vessel of the fish' is the literal meaning." They walked down the cobblestone walkway next to the many budding rose bushes and lavender plants that were starting to bloom in the late winter sun. They passed a rock garden with what looked like an imitation Stonehenge.

"You'll have to educate me, Emma."

"It's very ancient. It's a symbol of the creation of man and woman, of god and goddess, of the intersection of the divine and the earthly realms of reality."

"Is this a Christian thing?" he asked.

"The Christians used it for their own purposes, but a simpler way of putting it is—as above, so below. Everyone is equal. I think I'm going to like your friend, Samuel. This tells me we see the universe in the same way. I need her right now."

They reached a second wooden door at the end of the cobblestone walkway and Samuel rang another bell. There was another release, and he opened the door. They went inside, where the wall to their immediate right was painted with giant red hibiscus flowers. Next to it was a quote by Walt Whitman painted in black lettering on a white background extolling the virtues of people who give back to society. It read:

> This is what you shall do; Love the earth and sun and the animals, despise riches, give alms to every one that asks, stand up for the stupid and crazy, devote your income and labor to others, hate tyrants, argue not concerning God, have patience and indulgence toward the people, take off your hat to nothing known or unknown or to any man or number of men, go freely with powerful uneducated persons and with the young and with the mothers of families, read these leaves in the open air every season of every year of your life, re-examine all you have been told at school or church or in any book, dismiss whatever insults your own soul, and your very flesh shall be a great poem and have the richest fluency not only in its words but in the

silent lines of its lips and face and between the lashes of your eyes and in every motion and joint of your body.

"He speaks the truth," said Emma.

The house lay on the other side of a small swimming pool and fenced yard. On the left side of the house constellations from the night sky were painted. On the right side a red brick wall stood above several vacant spaces for medicinal plants with nameplates. Overlooking the garden and the medicinal plants was a bust of Merlin, the medieval magician, perhaps suggesting that the plants could be used to cast spells. Above the statue of the magician was a lone bamboo pole, and dangling from it, a crystal bell tinkled in the wind.

Over the front door there was a small brass bell. Obviously Ana Cejas knew they were present because she had buzzed them through two gates. But it seemed important and equally symbolic that they ring the bell as a way of acknowledging that they had wandered through her magical garden and taken in some of its wonders.

The therapist was petite, with streaked blond hair and welcoming blue eyes. She extended both hands and took Emma's in hers. "You're right on time, Emma. Welcome. Samuel speaks marvels of you."

"Thank you so much for seeing me," said Emma.

"I will leave you two together," said Samuel. "Thank you for your help, Ana."

He squeezed Emma's hand and left, walking back through the lovely garden, out the first gate, down the cobblestone walkway, and finally out the gate of the interlocking circles, closing it behind him.

Inside, Ana took a distressed Emma and sat her down in one of two rocking chairs that faced each other in her consultation room.

"There's no agenda here, Emma. I'm here to help you," said a sympathetic Ana. "Tell me a little about yourself."

Emma couldn't. All she could do was weep. Ana sat quietly and rocked back and forth as Emma cried for the entire fifty minutes of her visit. When time was up, Ana said, "Can we meet the day after tomorrow at the same time?"

"Yes, I will have to rearrange my schedule a little, but I like the idea of talking with you," she smiled faintly, "not that I have talked much, have I?"

"That's fine, Emma. I want you to think of three things that you wish to accomplish for yourself in our meetings."

"All I want I right now and forever is the safe return of my son," said Emma.

Ana held up her hand. "I know that, Emma, and we will work on that every time we are together. You need to go beyond that, as painful as it may be for you. I want to know the three things that you personally want to accomplish with our meetings. Please take this essential oil with you. It's chamomile. It helps you focus when things seem out of sorts. Put it in this clay amphorita and put it around your neck. Smell it during the day when you are troubled." She handed her a small bottle of oil, along with a card with her phone number. "I will see you in two days," she said.

6

We Need a Profile

While Emma was with Ana Cejas, Samuel barged into Bernardi's office.

"We've been at this for two days and two nights, Bruno, and so far we've come up with nothing. We need to work on a profile of this psychopath The longer that kid is out there, the less chance he stays alive. Tell me what you've found out," said Samuel.

"There are a lot of yellow VW buses registered in the Bay Area, but that doesn't mean much."

"You mean because driving a bus gives him mobility," said Samuel. "So where do you think we go?"

"North, south, and east."

"In other words, we guess," said Samuel.

"We need to make an educated one, but we only get one shot at it. If we're wrong and the abductor is a killer, we're screwed. Before we do that you need to ask Emma some questions, and we may need some help from her psychologist."

"What do you mean?" asked Samuel.

"We need to know if someone from her past may be involved."

"What's the basis for that theory?"

"A lot of crimes like kidnapping stem from domestic

disputes."

"I don't see how that applies here. The father of the child was killed in Vietnam. Who's left?" asked Samuel.

"I don't know. It's just a thought, and maybe not even worth pursuing, but we might as well look into every option. I'd tell her you want to sit in on a session while she goes over her connections with people in her past."

* * *

Samuel made arrangements with Ana Cejas to see Emma the next day, even though she wasn't scheduled, and he got permission from both of them to sit in on the session. They again walked the short distance from Emma's home to Ana's house, rang the bell, and wandered through her magical garden to her consultation room. Samuel was given his own rocking chair, and the session began.

"Emma, you know that what happens here between us is entirely confidential. But he asked to sit in on this hour, and you consented."

"Yes, Samuel is trying to help me, and I know that," she said sadly as she rocked in her chair.

"Let's get started then."

Ana lit a bundle of sage and walked quickly around the room, allowing the smoke to linger in the air. She put it down and took her seat by a statue of Quan Yin, the Chinese Goddess of Mercy.

Ana asked for a short account of Emma's early life with an emphasis on memorable people.

Emma's voice was weak, her eyes were red with bags underneath. She said that her early childhood had been a lonely time. She explained that her mother died in giving birth to her. Janus, her father, had lost his country of Poland to the Germans during the war and after that to the Soviets. Her father tried to raise her within the Catholic Church as a way of protecting her and giving her structure. He worked long hours as a mechanic in the coal mines. His weekends were taken up with household chores and the Church, which was a part of the fabric of the town. He accepted the rules as delivered from the pulpit and tried to make sure that she lived with the fear of God firmly instilled in her.

"He realized he could not raise me by himself, so he was grateful for the help he received from my maternal grandmother. She at least provided a feminine touch and some guidance in my early life."

Emma explained that she had been a very introverted child but found a saving grace in art. "I was told I was a keen observer, and that I had inherited that gift from him, my father. I was told I exhibited it from early on. I drew butterflies at first. By eight, horses fascinated me, and people said I could capture their strength and magical force with a few pencil strokes. At eleven, I mustered up my courage and started drawing portraits. When I drew people on paper, my teachers told me it was remarkable how I could capture emotion and energy, and how I could remember the nuances of features after only momentary glances. That gave me confidence.

"I always fantasized about my mother and had constant visions of her face. These were reinforced by the lone photograph that existed at my grandmother's house. I refined every detail of her in my drawings, and once I started, I created an outpouring of idealized portraits.

"My father did what he could to help me. He would take me for walks in the woods with my sketchpad, and we would talk about the bugs I saw or a bird that was sitting on the fence or darting through the air as we approached. I drew almost everything I saw and surprised my father with my eye for details.

"You want to know about important people in my past,

and I'm sorry that I've taken so long to get to this. This is not something I like to talk about." She explained she was fifteen when she met Professor Maurice Levantine, an accomplished portrait painter. During the war he had collaborated with the Germans, and as a result, after it was over, he spent some years in prison. Upon his return he slowly reintegrated into the town and once again became a successful portraitist.

"From early on, he had his eye on me. He would often engage me in conversation and examine my drawings. He told me I was talented and that my drawings were lovely.

"Over a period of a few months, Professor Levantine established a relationship with me. He first asked me to sit for him in the little studio where he lived. It all started innocently enough, and I posed for him on three different occasions. Then the atmosphere changed. The professor tendered me a daisy during the course of one afternoon when I was sitting on the stool. We then started to pull the petals from it, one by one, and he chanted the mantra, 'She loves me, she loves me not.' His eyes twinkled as he lightly touched my hand.

"The next time I posed for him, he asked me to remove my blouse so he could better see the curves of my shoulders. As he helped me remove it, his hand brushed up against my breast, and I noted that my nipples were erect against my slip."

On that occasion he talked with her for an hour or so, and while sketching recounted the lives of several impressionist painters. "I listened very carefully, moved both by the stories of creativity and his soft voice. The professor bided his time. He frequently repositioned me during the sitting, making sure his hand brushed up against my breast or lingered on one of my shoulders.

"After several sittings in my slip, he suggested that he would like to draw me in the nude from the waist up. I remember I blushed, but excitement raced through me. Since I was halfway under the professor's spell, I saw no harm in his artistic endeavor with me as a model. He often compared my beauty to many of the ancient Greek and Roman goddesses. Pretty hard for a young lonely girl to ignore, I must tell you.

"Levantine continued this slow manipulation until he was ready to strike. On a sunny afternoon several weeks later, I was seated on a stool, bare from the waist up, and he was talking about the connection between poetry and what it stimulates in the person who listens to and understands it. He moved to my side and repositioned me again, brushing against my naked breast, and I remember that my nipples hardened again as I became visibly excited. He took my hand and kissed it and moved his lips up my arm while caressing my breasts. I didn't know exactly what was about to happen, but I could not resist either."

"Do you want me to step outside?" asked Samuel, also embarrassed at having to listen in on something so private and intimate.

"If you would please wait out there until I finish this part," said Emma, openly crying at what she was disclosing.

Samuel walked out into Ana's garden and occupied himself re-reading Walt Whitman's quote on the wall.

Emma continued her story, relieved that she didn't have to reveal it in front of Samuel. "He moved me off the stool and placed me on a nearby cot. I blushed as he kissed my breasts and licked my neck, while rubbing my legs and buttocks. He then moved his right hand up my leg and started feeling my sex through my panties. I was wet. He moved my panties aside and started massaging my clitoris, which had become erect and hard as a pebble. I was still a virgin, but I had been sexually excited when riding a horse or jumping up and down on a fence rail, and lately, since he had begun to appreciate my body, I had been touching myself."

"That is a lot to put a young girl through," said Ana.

"Thank you, Ana. It is hard to let this out, and I appreciate your help. The professor lifted my skirt and inserted his tongue in my sex. He soon had me groaning with delight. Something I hate to admit."

"I understand that, Emma. Don't worry. It is very human of you to feel that way."

"He then climbed on top and penetrated me. I felt a sharp pain and cried with agony and fright, but it was over very soon. There was now blood on the cover of the cot. I cried softy as the professor caressed me and held me in his arms, reassuring me that everything was all right, that I was a wonderful girl, and that next time I would feel the same pleasure that he did.

"The experience was confusing to me. My strict Catholic upbringing clashed with these new sensuous yearnings. I was torn between the two sides of my nature, the pious and the lustful one. I longed to talk with my mother, whom I feared was looking down on me with disapproval, not imagining for a moment that she would do anything but castigate me, never suspecting it was she who had actually seduced my father. While such a confidence might have made me feel better at the time, it wouldn't have made any difference, since at my age, raging hormones won the battle.

"Professor Levantine never rushed me. During the next six months we were together twice a week, and he taught me many things about lovemaking. I opened my soul to my mentor and gave myself totally to him, the way only a teenage girl could. The affection of the professor started to heal the wound of my mother's death. Soon his den was the only place where I felt at ease. I even added feminine touches by purchasing embroidered doilies at village fairs and placing them around the small studio, or by bringing fresh flowers."

"Can we ask Samuel back in, Emma?"

"Yes, he should hear the rest."

Samuel took a chair discreetly and Emma continued.

"One afternoon, I had broken my routine and was in the

vicinity of the professor's bungalow. I lightly knocked before entering, and what I encountered dumbfounded me. Professor Levantine was in bed, naked, with the waitress from the café.

"I ran from the apartment down the stairs and on to the street. I raced to the woods on the edge of the little town, and I found a brook deep in the woods where I collapsed, in deep pain over this betrayal."

"I'm really sorry," interrupted Samuel. "This mentor of yours was French, wasn't he?"

"Yes, of course," she said.

"Did this person wear a beard?" asked Samuel.

Emma looked up, startled. "Why, yes, he did."

"What kind of music did you listen to with him, if you remember?"

"He loved Debussy and Wagner, I remember that."

"Do you know if this man ever came to the United States?" asked Samuel.

"I heard that he did, but I've never seen him."

"After your child was born, did he ever contact you?"

"He tried, but I wouldn't talk to him, so I just assumed that he gave up."

"Can you give me a description?"

"Taller than you are, with a good build, brown hair, and with a kind of a beard—I'm not sure what you would call it. But this was a long time ago."

"Does the word goatee mean anything to you?" asked Samuel.

Emma shook her head.

"Let me make sure I understand you. You heard he came to the U.S., but you never saw him?"

"That's right," said Emma. "He tried to contact me many times. He told me that he was very much in love with me, but I wanted nothing to do with him. When I came to the United States with Ian, I lost track of him."

"Excuse me," said Samuel. "I have to make a quick exit. I may want to repeat this at some time in the future, if you don't mind," he said to both Emma and Ana.

"It's up to Emma," said Ana.

Emma nodded. "I want to help in any way I can."

"Thank you, Emma. This really helps." Samuel was off.

7

Alain Comes Back to Life

ALAIN WOKE UP GROGGY and disoriented. He didn't know how much time had lapsed since he was taken. He found himself lying on a green canvas army cot surrounded by four white padded walls. His mouth felt like it was full of cotton. He didn't know where he was, but from the light outside and the chill in the air, he figured it was early in the morning. He threw up and noticed that there was vomit on the rug that extended from underneath the only door to his bedside. There was a small window high up on the wall and an intercom in the ceiling. There was also a slop bucket in the corner near a small door that could be used for taking it away or replacing it from the outside. A bear rug covered part of the floor.

Alain was an unusual boy from birth. Extremely inquisitive, he seemingly inherited his grandfather's and his father's aptitudes for abstract mathematics and eclectic interests. He bonded closely with his mother and his adopted grandmother Reyna, and they watched after him, encouraging him to pursue any subject that interested him. As a young child, he followed the leads of his grandfather, Janus Olech, and his father, Ian Sheridan, both of whom loved to build things. He didn't mix well with the outside world and didn't like to be touched by strangers. He focused strongly when he was interested in a subject and had read everything he could about survival and wilderness training. For the most part he was unfriendly to other children his own age. People described him as standoffish.

He could hear the noise of the waves crashing on rocks in the distance, and so he knew he was near the ocean. It took him a few minutes to try and clear his head, but he couldn't get rid of the nausea. When he saw the tray of food inside the door, he moved as quickly as he could to the slop bucket and threw up again. Afterwards he sat cross-legged on the floor and tried to gather his thoughts.

When his stomach felt settled enough, he removed the cloth covering from the tray and saw a glass of orange juice, a bowl of what he thought was yogurt, and a small jar of Pepto-Bismol. He wasn't sure if it was safe, so he didn't touch any of it. He crawled to the slop bucket and retched again. He took the cot and stood it on end, thinking he could climb it and look out the window, but in his haze, he couldn't figure out how to secure it so it wouldn't fall.

He jumped at a crackling noise. He looked in the direction from which it was coming and realized it was from the speaker in the ceiling. He heard a voice coming out of it. "Bonjour, Alain. I hope you had a restful night," it said in French.

"Who are you? And what I am doing here? And where am I?" he responded in French.

"We'll deal with all these questions in due time. First you must get settled. Take what time you need," the voice answered.

"I need something for my stomach. It is very upset."

"That is why I left the yogurt and the Pepto-Bismol. They will help you with the nausea. It will take a couple of days."

"I don't trust you, and you left the yogurt, the orange juice, and the medicine in the wrong order. They need to be placed in the order I want them, which is the Pepto-Bismol first."

"I don't have any idea what you're talking about," said Maurice. "I mean you no harm. As soon as you are feeling better, we will talk. I will explain everything."

Alain was frightened and sick. But he was a boy of strict routines, so he concentrated on calming down. He had been warned many times never to trust a stranger and never to go anywhere with one. He knew he was in trouble, and he needed to think clearly, but right now his stomach was too upset. He decided to try and get well and then figure things out. He set the cot back down and put a blanket on top of it. He then lay down, covered himself with another blanket, and went back to sleep, hoping that the nausea would subside.

8

A Shot in the Dark

"I WANT TO CHECK OUT if any VWs in the state are registered to a Maurice Levantine," said Samuel.

"Who is that?" asked Bernardi.

Samuel explained what he learned in his conversation with Emma. "I know it's a long shot, but we're desperate, and time is against us."

"Spell the name for me."

When he had what needed, Bernardi got on the phone, told the officer what information to get from the Department of Motor Vehicles, and asked how long it would take.

As the person on the other end of the line responded, Bernardi put a hand over the receiver. "He said he will have something for me in half an hour, but we shouldn't stop there. We should also cover car leasing companies."

"This guy is from France, I think I should also contact Perkins so we can get information from Immigration."

"Oh, shit. That guy Perkins again," said Bernardi. "Why don't we just turn this over to Patruski? It's his case unless the worst happens."

"This one is too personal for me to have it in someone else's hands," said Samuel. "I'll make the contact with Perkins myself, as soon as we hear from the DMV."

53

Within the half hour, they had the information that there was in fact a VW bus registered to a Maurice Levantine at a San Francisco address.

"Let's go," said Samuel.

"Wait a minute. We need a warrant, and we need Patruski to come with us." Bernardi got on the phone and arranged for a warrant and had his officers find Patruski and tell him to get to homicide immediately. In addition, he put out an all-points bulletin for Maurice Levantine.

* * *

A couple of hours later with a warrant in hand, Bernardi, Patruski, Mac, and Samuel headed to the Telegraph Hill address given by the DMV for Maurice Levantine in San Francisco. Three squad cars accompanied them with armed sheriff officers. Patruski banged on the apartment door and got no response. Two officers broke it down. The entourage entered with Patruski in the lead with his hand gun drawn and Bernardi and Mac following closely behind. Samuel waited for the officers to clear the apartment before he ventured inside.

Once they had searched the two-bedroom apartment for any occupants, they gathered in the living room with its spectacular view of Treasure Island and the Bay Bridge. "Sergeant Patruski, this is still your case," said Bernardi, "but we all have a stake in it, so I'm here just in case it turns into another nightmare. What do you want us to do?"

"Let's take a careful look around and see what we can find," said Patruski. "The first thing to do is see if this guy could have left something that will tell us where he's gone. Let's start in the bedroom."

The whole crowd moved to the bedroom, and opened all the dresser drawers and took all the clothes out of the closet, tore the bed linen apart but found nothing.

"Let's split up," said Bernardi. "Mac and I will take the kitchen. Have one of your officers get hold of the landlord and find out if there's a storage unit connected to this place."

Patruski didn't like being second fiddle on a kidnapping case, so he offered to contact the landlord. He was gone about ten minutes when he returned with the building manager. "This is Mr. Giancomo. Each tenant has a storage room. I suggest we follow him downstairs after you gentlemen are through with the kitchen."

The landlord looked at the shattered door. "Why didn't you call me before you did this? I could have let you in."

"We're sorry, it's an emergency," said Bernardi. "We didn't know if your tenant was hiding in there, and we didn't have time to go and get you. He wasn't in there, and we're searching the place, but with your help we'll go and search his storeroom. We can come back to this later. Please help us, Mr. Giancomo. Lead the way."

Bernardi's words calmed down the manager, and he led them down to the basement to Levantine's storage room. It had a padlock on it.

"Do you have a key to this?" asked Patruski.

"No, sir," said the manager.

He motioned to Mac, who took out a bolt cutter and snipped off the lock. Patruski, Bernardi, and Mac entered the room and turned on the light. There was a treasure trove of evidence, including tape, rope, and chloroform.

"These by themselves don't prove anything," said Patruski, "but taken together, they can be strong circumstantial evidence against this man."

Samuel, who was behind the others, chimed in, "Can you see if there's anything that shows where he might have taken the boy?"

They looked for a map or any other piece of evidence which would point to the victim's whereabouts, but found nothing.

55

"Can we go back upstairs and see if he had a desk or some other place where he kept what he considered important papers?" asked Samuel.

Patruski sent Mac with Samuel back to the apartment to see if such evidence existed. They went directly to the bedroom to check the desk that had not been searched. Mac began to open the drawers. He had gloves on and took out old opened envelopes, one by one. There were mostly bills that were marked paid, with the date of payment noted in ink.

"What's that one?" asked Samuel.

"It's from the U.S. Department of Labor. It's a confirmation of a mining claim by Mr. Maurice Levantine in the Big Sur area of California."

"I think that's important," said Samuel. "Can you take a photo of it? I'll run down and get Bernadi and Patruski."

"Will do," answered Mac.

Samuel rushed downstairs and brought Patruski and Bernardi back with him. "Remember this guy's got a bus, so he can go anywhere. He could hide out in an abandoned mine," Samuel said pointing to the letter from the U.S. Department of Labor.

"I get what you're thinking," said Bernardi.

Patruski shook his head. "Let's see if we can get the Feds to cooperate with us."

Samuel interrupted, "I have a source that can help us if we need it."

Bernardi rolled his eyes but didn't say anything.

"Let me give them a call," said Patruski. "I'll know this afternoon."

"Wait a minute," said Mac. "There's a claim number. I doubt if we'll have any trouble with them giving us information on where to find this on a map."

"Okay, I'll radio this back to the Department. We should know something by the time we get back downtown. In fact,

I'll leave you all right now while you finish up. I should have something pretty quick," said Patruski.

* * *

With the description of Levantine and the location of the mining claim in the Big Sur area, Patruski got a warrant from Monterey County. He made arrangements to meet the Monterey County deputy sheriff the next day. Patruski, Bernardi, Mac, and Samuel all went in one car. Another van followed with Mac's forensic team. The drive took them almost four hours. They met the deputy in the parking lot of the Nepenthe Restaurant in Big Sur. The caravan of vehicles climbed the coastal mountain to the claim, parked in the space by the cabin. It looked abandoned, but there were fresh tire marks leading to and from the car park area. An outbuilding, downhill from what looked like the main residence, faced the ocean with wooden stairs leading to it.

"This doesn't look much like a mining claim," said Patruski.

"People use these places as vacation homes and weekend getaways," said the deputy in charge of serving the warrant. "There hasn't been any gold discovered here for a long time."

The deputy and his men knocked on the cabin door, but there was no answer. They peered in the side windows. Then two of them broke down the front door and entered the single story structure. The entire group of some ten men filed into the place. There was a fireplace, a small kitchen, a desk with a microphone on it, a single bed in the corner with a patched quilt covering it, and a dresser with drawers that had been left open but were empty.

"It looks like whoever was here left in a hurry," said Samuel.

"Let's take a look in the other place that's down the hill," said the deputy.

57

They all filed out of the front door of the cabin, and the deputy led the way down the flight of stairs to the outbuilding below. Again, he knocked on the door, but there was no answer. He and his men then knocked the door in. It had three deadbolts on it that were not easy to dismantle.

Patruski watched intently as the job was completed. "How about letting our forensic team in there before anyone else?" he said.

The deputies moved aside. Patruski and Mac entered with Bernardi and Samuel by their sides. A green army cot was propped on end underneath a high window. Scuff marks indicated that someone had used the cot to get up to the window. The glass was broken and the frame was ripped out of it. Part of it was on the floor. A blanket was tied to the legs of the cot. One end hung out the window. It was obvious that someone had used it to leave the room. There was an empty slop bucket by the door.

"If the kid was here, I wonder if he made it?" said Patruski.

Mac started taking photographs as his assistant took fingerprints from every part of the room and from the slop bucket.

"Let's check the outside to see if there is any signs he got away," said Patruski. He and Bernardi and Samuel and one of the deputies went further down the hill on the outside of the building. The blanket hanging out of the window was tied to another one with a substantial knot. Its end hung about five feet above the ground. Marks on the hillside showed that whoever had used the blanket made it out of the building and slid a few feet downhill. Then, some strange footprints left the area, almost as if they were from Bigfoot.

"It had to be the boy. It looks like he fastened some kind of footwear made out of cloth, and that's why the footprints look so big. That could mean he escaped," said Patruski. "He must have tried to cover his escape route because he brushed any evidence of where he was going just a few feet down the hill," and he pointed to where the tracks became undecipherable.

"Is there any indication that he was followed?" asked Samuel.

"Yeah, right next to the oversized ones, you see the print of what looks like an adult boot, but it doubles back once the tracks disappear. We don't actually know if he got away or got caught. I'd better get Mac down here to get plaster of Paris impressions of these," said Patruski.

"I'll get him for you," said Samuel, and he climbed back up the hill to the door of the outbuilding. "Mac, they need you down the hill to make some casts of footprints."

Mac left with one of the technicians and a bag full of material. Alone in the room, Samuel looked carefully at what was left. He figured that the boy must have used three blankets to get out of the room by tying them together and making a rope that extended outside. He knew that Mac and the other technicians would get all the clues that were available, and he walked outside and yelled for Bernardi. "Can we take a look at the main cabin and see if there is anything that gives a hint where the kidnapper might have gone to hide or even have taken the boy, if he caught him?"

Bernardi talked it over with Patruski and came up the hill. "Let's take a look."

Samuel and Bernardi went into the main cabin where everything was in shambles indicating that the place had been left in a hurry. Samuel looked underneath the bed. Nothing. He opened all the cupboards, noting that everything had been taken. There wasn't even an empty tube of toothpaste in the wastebasket.

"What about the trash cans?" said Samuel.

They went outside and looked in the car park where there were two containers that had been animal proofed. Samuel opened them up, one by one, but they were both empty.

"I'll make sure Mac gets prints off of them," said Bernardi.

Samuel took another look at the main cabin. Above the front door there had been some kind of a placard. The place had a name, he thought, but it had been ripped off. He pointed this out to Bernardi. "If we could find out what he called this place, we might have a clue to his whereabouts," he said.

"Okay," said Bernardi. "Get to work, and find out."

It was already dark by five o'clock when the group met at the front door to the main cabin. They loaded several bags of articles that had been collected on the site, packing them into the forensic team's van.

"Does anybody think we need to stay in the area until tomorrow just in case we forgot anything?" asked Patruski.

"I'd like to rent a car and spend the night somewhere nearby," said Samuel.

"I'll stay with you," said Bernardi.

"I'd stay too," said Patruski, "but I have to process all this evidence. We already have an all-points bulletin out for this Levantine guy. This is a small community, so I doubt if he'll get very far from here unless he's already left the area."

The Monterey County deputy sheriff drove Samuel and Bernardi to the outskirts of Carmel where Samuel was able to rent a car. A bit later he and Bernardi bought toothbrushes and razors. The three of them had a bite to eat at a fish restaurant in Carmel Valley. "Will you go back to Big Sur with us, so we can look over other possibilities where this suspect might be hiding?" asked Samuel.

The deputy agreed, and the three of them went back to Big Sur to the Sheriff's substation to go over the list of claim cabins that were designated as possible break-in sites. Samuel wrote down the names of several that he wanted to ask about when he hooked up with the Bureau of Land Management.

He knew that state or county officials didn't have the specific detail he was looking for, but he also knew that they were in a race against time. They drove to several sites on the mountainside. All were closed for the winter, and none gave the appearance of having been recently inhabited or disturbed. Samuel didn't find the special name he was looking for, either.

After several hours of prowling around, they decided to call it quits until the next morning. The officer agreed to meet them at 7:00 A.M. Samuel and Bernardi checked into a local motel in Big Sur. It was now well after midnight. Samuel contemplated calling Emma but decided not to because he had no good news to give her, and he didn't want to say anything that she could interpret as bad. He did have some questions he needed to ask her, but he wanted to think about how to phrase them so that she wouldn't get alarmed.

As soon as Samuel hit the pillow in the small motel room, he fell asleep, and had his recurrent nightmare. He was behind the wheel of a car, drunk and driving erratically when all of a sudden a young woman appeared out of nowhere. Because of his speed and his intoxication he couldn't stop. He struck her. Samuel woke up bathed in a cold sweat. He hadn't had the dream for some time—in fact, not since he'd gotten over his depression—but it was back.

At six o'clock in the morning, he called Emma and woke her up. "We're pretty sure Maurice Levantine kidnapped your son, but it looks like Alain escaped from the cabin where he had him hidden."

"Why on earth would he do something like that?" she exclaimed with horrified anguish.

"That's what we're trying to find out, but we won't know for sure until we find him. We're on his trail right now. We feel he's around here somewhere close."

"I can't believe it, Samuel. That man hasn't bothered me for years. I have had absolutely nothing to do with him other than what I described to the therapist in your presence."

"I'm sure of that, Emma. Let me just assure you again that we think Alain escaped, and we also think that Maurice is looking for him, but I wouldn't be surprised if Alain outsmarted him. Let me ask you a few questions that may help us catch him."

* * *

Bernardi got Charles Perkins' home number through police headquarters, and Samuel was on the phone with him.

The sleepy prosecutor answered. "Charles, this is Samuel. I'm in a bind down here in Monterey County, and I need your help."

"What the hell is wrong with you, Samuel? Calling me at this ungodly hour?"

Samuel explained to him that they were on the trail of a kidnapper and described what they found at the abandoned mining claim. He told Charles what he needed from him.

"All I can say is that you're lucky that an innocent child is involved. Otherwise, I'd tell you to get screwed."

"Thanks, Charles. Can I call you back around noon?"

"Call my office. All you really want me to do is grease the wheels for you to access the information. If I'm not there, my secretary will tell you who to contact. And when you write the story remember to mention where you got the information."

"I always take care of you, Charles, you know that," said Samuel.

"Not always, you bastard."

"That again?" said Samuel. "You're covered, I promise."

Samuel, Bernardi and the deputy spent the rest of the morning going over site maps of the vast Big Sur area, which covered ninety miles of coastline and extended inland some twenty-one miles to the San Lucia mountains. They saw the various dots on the map the Sheriff's department had gotten from the Federal Government, but they acknowledged it would take months to go to all the potential mine sites spread throughout the area. All waited with anticipation until noon when Samuel was supposed to be back in touch with Perkins' office.

Shortly after noon Samuel called, and Perkins' secretary gave him a name and a phone number of a contact at the Bureau of Land Management office in San Francisco.

Samuel immediately got hold of Donald Haas, who was in charge of the San Francisco office. "Mr. Haas, my name is Samuel Hamilton. I'm a friend of Charles Perkins, as you know, and I'm down here in Big Sur helping the SFPD on a kidnapping case. We've just been to the cabin of Maurice Levantine, the main suspect in the case, and it was abandoned, but we have reason to believe that he has another cabin in these mountains. We need your help to locate it."

"The claim he keeps current with us is the one you were at last night, if I understood Mr. Perkins correctly. He has it registered under the name of Maurice Levantine."

"All right. How about another claim under his name in the same area?"

"I checked that and there is none."

"How about another claim that's registered by him under a German name?"

"I will have to check that. Can you hold for a minute?"

"Go ahead," said Samuel, and he cupped the phone.

"What made you think of asking about a German name?" asked Bernardi.

"Emma told me he was a collaborator with the Germans during the war, and even went to prison when it was over."

Haas came back on the phone. "We'll have to do some more checking. It will take a couple of hours. Can you call me back?"

63

"Sure. If he registered it in another name, wouldn't he have to prove he was that person?" asked Samuel.

"Yes, he would. But once he was on record with one claim, he could register it in his wife's name or he could give the claim a German name, as you suggest. We see that often, especially with Spanish titles. People have romantic ideas about the old days, and they play with them."

Later that day, Samuel was on the phone again to Donald Haas. "Any luck?"

"Interesting question, Mr. Hamilton. We did a little research and we have a claim filed in the name of Friedrich der Grosse. He calls it *Himmel auf Erden.* One of my staff who speaks German says this has to be a joke because Friedrich der Grosse is Frederick the Great. But more interesting is that it also belongs to Maurice Levantine. It's only a couple of miles away from the one you were at yesterday."

"What does the claim name mean?"

"Himmel auf Erden means Heaven on Earth."

"Interesting. I'll have to think about that one."

"How did you figure out that we'd find another one?"

"It's a complicated story. Some time I'll tell you. Right now, we have to get up there while it's still daylight. Can you give me the specifics?" He wrote the claim number and all the information that Haas gave him on a separate sheet of paper. "Hold on. How do we get there? Give the particulars to the deputy," and Samuel turned the phone over to him.

The deputy asked several questions of Haas and wrote down his responses on the same sheet of paper that Samuel had written the claim number on. When he finished, he gave the phone back to Samuel.

"Thanks for all your help, Mr. Haas. I'll let you know how this turns out."

The deputy went over to the site map and pointed to the claim on it, and with a pencil traced how they could get there.

"I need to call for backup, just in case we find this nut there. But that complicates things because I'd like to get there while it's still daylight."

"We need the backup," said Bernardi. "All we know is that we're dealing with a kidnapper and maybe a murderer."

The deputy got on the phone to Monterey and talked briefly to someone. "It will take them thirty to forty minutes. Sorry to delay it further but it could be dangerous for everyone if we don't have the right protection."

"Do you think we need a warrant?" asked Samuel.

"Of course not," said Bernardi. "We're pursing a felon. This is the same guy that kidnapped the kid."

After four o'clock the caravan of sheriff's deputies together with Samuel and Bernardi were ready. The deputies led the way up the steep and narrow mountain road beside the towering pines to the claim site. Looking down the mountain they saw a faded yellow Volkswagen bus under a well-constructed wood carport. Just above the door of the cabin was a wood crafted sign that they couldn't read from where they had stopped. Samuel and Bernardi, who were behind the sheriff's cars, were relieved when they saw the outline of the bus.

Everyone got out of their cars and all eight of them gathered in front of the first sheriff's car. Three men had shotguns, and all had side arms except for Samuel. The captain in charge of the sheriff's deputies spoke first. "My plan is to surround the cabin and then with a megaphone demand that the occupants come out with their hands up. If we don't get a response, we'll have to break down the door and take them by force."

"Our only concern is that if the boy is there and the kidnapper feels trapped, he may do him harm," said Bernardi.

"The problem is that we don't want to just surround the place and play a waiting game with this character, especially if it turns out that that the boy's not there."

"I think that at least the kidnapper is there," said Samuel.

"He couldn't get very far without his bus, so I say let's surround the place and tell him to come out."

"I admit he's an unknown entity, but we can't wait around all night or even starve him out," said the captain. The armed deputies surrounded the cabin, two on each of three sides, with the captain, Bernardi, and Samuel at the front door. Above the door was the now familiar sign Himmel auf Erden. The captain knocked at the door. The windows on both sides of the cabin were high enough off the ground so that the inside of the cabin couldn't be seen from outside except at a distance. The smell of freshly baked bread wafted through the air. "This is Captain Gerald Lancer of the Monterey County Sheriff's Office," he said through the battery operated megaphone. "Open the door and show yourself with your hands in the air." There was no answer.

The captain repeated his order once more. Then he and another deputy used a battering ram, hitting the door three times, knocking it down. Both moved quickly inside with guns drawn while other deputies went around the sides of the cabin.

They found themselves in a modest living room with a high ceiling. There were potatoes in a bubbling pot on the stove and bread baking in the oven, but no people. Bernardi turned the stove and the oven off.

In the rear of the cabin on the down slope, there was a commotion. Samuel ran out the front door and down the side where deputies were struggling with a tall gray-headed man with a well-trimmed beard. He was muscular and giving them quite a battle. "Don't shoot him," cried Samuel. "We need him to find the boy."

The man and three of the deputies rolled down the mountainside, grappling with each other in the fading light of the late afternoon. Blood spurted out of a cut on Levantine's head, and a deputy had a huge welt on his forehead from head-butting the kidnapper. Finally, some fifty feet further down the slope, the deputies subdued and handcuffed him. By that time, Samuel was by their side. "Where's Alain?" he yelled. "You have to tell us! Your life depends on it."

There was no answer. The man seemed dazed and befuddled. "How did you find me?" was all he said.

Samuel realized that his approach wasn't going to work on the kidnapper.

Captain Lancer, Bernardi, and the other deputies were soon at the capture site.

"We need to know what you did with the boy," scowled Bernardi. There was still no answer.

"Okay, you're under arrest for the kidnapping of Alain Sheridan. If you want to save your skin, you'd better start talking," said Bernardi.

"Let's get him back up the hill."

Once they had the prisoner back in the cabin and seated in an armchair, the questioning resumed. The smell of baked bread still lingered. Bernardi went over everything with him that was known about his past in France, his relationship with Emma, his prison time after the war for being a quisling to the German war occupation of France, and his coming to the U.S. in the late 1950s.

Maurice looked at the group of officers and at Samuel as if they were ghosts, or as if he were an alien from another planet. He kept shaking his head and either pretending he didn't understand what was going on or refusing to believe that his plan to steal Alain had been foiled. His interrogators couldn't tell which.

"Just tell us where the boy is," pleaded Bernardi, who was a skilled interrogator. "We need to know that he's safe."

Again, there was no response.

Bernardi called Captain Lancer outside. Samuel was with them, while Maurice was guarded inside the cabin by the remaining deputies. "I'm willing to push this guy all night, if I have to, but we also need to make arrangements to get him to San Francisco. Can you radio your command post to have SFPD send a unit to your substation in Monterey? They'll need to transport him to county jail in San Francisco when I'm through with him."

"We'll take care of that right now," said the captain.

Samuel and Bernardi returned to the cabin while the captain went to his patrol car to relay the message.

Once inside the cabin Bernardi turned on his tape recorder and began to methodically question the accused. "You have to listen carefully, Maurice. You're in a lot of trouble. We know that you kidnapped Alain from 24th Street a few days ago. Your bus was identified as being at the scene and having made a U-turn immediately afterwards. We know that Alain was held captive in your other cabin and maybe even in this one. But he's not here now. So you need to tell us where we can find him. It will become very important in terms of how we treat you, and to an extent whether we can actually protect you. Inmates don't like kidnappers of children. They do awful things to people accused of these crimes."

Samuel, who was taking notes, tried to control the desperate tone in his voice and still make his point. "Lieutenant Bernardi is trying to help you, Maurice. We need to tell Alain's mother that he's alive and well. Won't you help us?"

For the first time, Maurice started to talk. He had a pained expression on his face and tears in his eyes. "Alain is my son. I conceived him with Emma. He is my only heir, and I was within my rights in taking him. That's because his mother betrayed me and would have nothing to do with me. She brought him to the United States without my permission. I've been trying to make connections with her and the boy since they got here, but she would not talk to me. I had to take this into my own hands because otherwise the boy would grow up not knowing who his real father is, and I would be deprived of my rightful heir." Samuel frowned, having heard Emma describe her relationship with him and how it had ended before she met Ian.

"There are still rules about spending time with children when you claim that they are your lawful issue," said Bernardi. "That is what our legal system is all about. But, you know, it doesn't allow kidnapping."

"I tried to reason with his mother, but she denied that I had anything to do with his being conceived."

"You're not on the birth certificate," said Samuel. "I've seen it. It says that Ian Sheridan is his father."

"That was just another of her conspiracies to deprive me of my lawful rights. She was angry with me about something that happened between us. I have forgiven her for that."

"That doesn't help you much right now," said Bernardi. "She was married to Ian Sheridan and since he was named as the father, the presumption is that he is the father."

"That is all legal mumbo jumbo," said Maurice. "I know my natural rights, and I was exercising them."

"All right, Maurice, just tell us what you did with the boy, and we'll deal with all these other issues in due course."

"I have nothing more to say."

"You won't tell us where he is. Is that what you're saying?" asked Samuel. "You realize that if something awful happened to him, it will be on you, don't you?"

The night dragged on but their captive stopped talking. Finally they concluded that they had to get moving. Bernardi turned over their prisoner to Captain Lancer. He and Samuel had to decide how to go about searching for Alain. Samuel needed to get to a telephone to call Emma and tell her that Maurice was the kidnapper, and he had been captured, but there was no sign of Alain.

It was past ten o'clock when they reached their motel in

Big Sur. Samuel got on the phone and talked with Emma and explained what had transpired with Maurice. He urged her to get an appointment with Ana Cejas for the next day, so she could get some emotional support. Then he touched the critical issue. "Do you think he would do Alain harm, even though he claims that he is his father?"

"I think that Maurice is a dishonest person, almost a crook, but unless he has changed dramatically, I don't think he would hurt Alain, or anybody else for that matter. But I have confidence in my son, Samuel. If he got away from Maurice, he will survive."

Samuel assured her that they would continue the search for Alain the next day. Once again, he didn't mention the other two kidnapped boys or the frightening possibility that Levantine might be guilty of three murders.

9

Who's the Father?

Emma couldn't wait to get to Ana Cejas' place to talk with her.

"I can't believe what that bastard said," Emma blurted out before she even said good morning.

"Let's start at the beginning," Ana counseled.

Trying to suppress her fits of anger, Emma recounted what Samuel had told her the previous evening. "The kidnapper claimed that he fathered Alain, and that was why he had taken him, because I had denied him access to his rightful heir."

"Is the kidnapper the same person who seduced you when you were fifteen?"

"Yes, the same person. Believe me, I haven't had anything to do with him since then. He must be demented to have concocted a story like the one he told the police. Ian Sheridan is Alain's father!"

"Tell me how you and Ian got together?"

"We met in Paris, in the street, actually. I was sketching a couple of runaways that hadn't bathed in weeks. They were sitting outside a bar begging for money for food."

"Did you like him immediately?"

"Very much. Ian was so attractive and vital. I didn't know how to respond to him, but we stumbled through our language barriers, and one thing led to another. After a party I invited him up to my place, but I told him that he would have to behave. I remember the stairway was narrow, and I went up first. Because of the poor light and the narrow confines, he bumped into me several times on the way up. I liked the contact and was waiting with anticipation for the next bump. He later told me he understood why I had the long slits in my skirt—without them I couldn't have made it up the narrow stairs.

"After the third landing, he put both hands on my buttocks and started caressing them. Then he quickly moved his hands around my waist and turned me to a sitting position on a stair riser. He kissed me, at first softly, then strongly. He was almost on top of me, and he began fondling my breasts with one hand as the other moved up and down my thigh until he reached my sex."

Ana, who was taking notes, looked up. "Did you want him to stop?"

"Yes. It was all too quick, too aggressive. Before I knew it, he had dropped his pants and was inside me.

"Even though he tried to hold up, he exploded in me. I was disgusted and angry. He was having trouble breathing, and I kept pushing him away.

"He asked me what was wrong, and he wanted to know if he had hurt me? He told me it was the most incredible experience he had ever had with a woman."

"Did you believe him?"

"Yes and no, but I was too upset to make sense of it all. I told him to just go. He asked when he could see me again. I needed time to think, so I told him that we would talk the following week, and he would know that I was home when the curtain was open. I lived on the fourth floor. My room had a small window with a light curtain that faced the street.

"When I got to my room, I was in tears. I lay on a little rug in the fetal position, rocking back and forth. My cat, Charbon, came over and licked the salty tears on my cheeks. All I could think of was Professor Levantine. I thought I was over the sorrow of that betrayal, but it all came back again in waves of pain and anger. I was on the floor for a long time. As I calmed down, I thought that I must have frightened Ian. I had really felt raped on the stairs, but I liked him. I would have felt different if it had happened under different circumstances. I couldn't decide if I wanted him or if it was better never to see him again."

Emma went on explaining. "On the appointed day I opened the curtain, and soon heard a tapping at my door. I opened it slowly and saw Ian standing there red-faced but smiling."

"Did you get pregnant from that experience with him?" asked Ana.

"I will get to that. First, let me tell you the rest of what happened. Ian came into my little apartment and we kissed on both cheeks and stood looking at each other in the middle of the room, both of us embarrassed. My radio was playing an Edith Piaf song. My place was a mess. In one corner next to the window, where the light was best, I had my easel. On the canvas was an incomplete human torso and head, almost classical in appearance, looking off into the distance. There were canvases and rolls of paper stacked in all available spaces and several paintings of my cat, Charbon, who was asleep in a basket near the little sink mid-distance on one of the walls.

"Ian explained that he didn't mean to hurt me. He asked for my forgiveness. He assured me that what had happened was not like him at all. He was not a brute. I told him that I was also very sorry and explained that there was more to my reaction than he could understand, but I couldn't bring myself to talk about it at that point. I said I wanted to give us another chance."

"What did he say?" asked Ana.

"He asked me to forgive him.

"I said I was capable of that, but it would take some time. I told him that I felt better talking, but he needed to understand how to treat a woman.

"We talked for over two hours. He wanted to take me to get something to eat. I wasn't ready but agreed to meet again.

"'I want to come and see you, Emma.'

"I kissed him on both cheeks and said good night.

"Over a week passed before I saw him again. And I was happy that he came to see me. I told him I had been thinking of him, wondering if he had disappeared. He held me at arm's length.

"'You look very cheerful,' he said.

"'What means cheerful?' I asked.

"'It means happy,' he said.

"I told him that I had been chosen to mount a show for my art school in Aix-en-Provence and asked him if he knew where that was. Of course, he didn't.

"I explained that Aix-en-Provence has a long history as a center for art and culture. It was an important center in France, and the Beaux-Arts school where I attended had a gallery there that showed the works of the students at the end of every school year. I was chosen to put the show together, and I even got to exhibit some of my own work.

"He asked if that meant I was famous.

"I laughed and explained that it just meant that I had to do all the dirty work that the professors didn't want to do. Cheap labor, I believe the Americans call it.

"'Where is Aix-en-Provence?' he asked.

"I told him it was in the southern part of the country, close to the Riviera. I took out a map and showed him that it was close to the city of Marseille.

"He offered to help me in setting up this show since he had time on his hands. So, we ended up in Aix-en-Provence together."

"Was this trip important in the development of your relationship with him?" asked Ana.

"Very important. That is where I really got to know him."

"Did you stay together in Aix-en-Provence?"

"No, but things happened there. After I was through with my work on the exhibit, we borrowed bicycles from students at the art school and went on a picnic. It was too hot at midday in August to enjoy the outdoors, so we waited until the afternoon cooled down and headed east toward Mt. Victoire.

"As we slowly climbed the lower slope of the mountain, I looked ahead at Ian and thought how much I liked him and how close to him I felt. About six o'clock, while the sun still lingered in the afternoon sky, we pulled our bicycles over to the side of the narrow road and took in the surroundings. There were sporadic fields of lavender interspersed with yellow patches of ground. I will never forget that place. I have painted it over and over again.

"Ian put his hand on my shoulder and pointed to what looked like a brook running between two lavender fields and surrounded by a small oasis of trees. It was at least a couple of kilometers away from the road we were on, but it looked accessible, so we pedaled our bikes down a dirt road until we got there. We spread a blanket on the ground near the stream. I unloaded the basket of food and laid it before him. Ian opened the bottle of wine and put it between two rocks in the brook. The aroma of lavender filled the air. I grabbed a handful and rubbed it in my hands and caressed Ian's face.

"Hungry after the long bike ride, we devoured one of the quiches and started on a roasted duck. Ian pulled the bottle of Côtes du Rhône out of the water and poured it into our glasses. We toasted and kissed, feeling deeply connected.

"At dusk, we enjoyed the golden hues of color that covered the sky as the sun disappeared behind the hills. Ian lay on the blanket with his head in my lap and we talked softly. I had tears in my eyes. He turned over and rose to his knees.

"'What's the matter, Emma?'

"'Nothing, Ian. I am very happy,' I told him.

"We kissed and embraced each other, and there was a mutual feeling of affection between us. We took our time, and made love for a long time. We whispered things to each other that I can still remember, and I have to admit it was one of the most beautiful experiences of my life. To this very moment I can still feel the emotions of that day and the closeness that I felt to him, and that I was sure he felt for me."

Emma's voice was dreamy as she recalled the experience. Ana sat quietly in her rocking chair while Quan Yin looked on benevolently.

"When we were satiated, we lay side by side, listening to the other sounds of the evening and the stream rushing by us as it slowly got dark. We continued talking and embracing until the moon was high in the sky.

"'Would you like to stay all night?' he asked.

"I answered that I would, but it would be cold, and the bugs would start to come out, and I had to pack things up at the exhibit. So we begrudgingly made our way back to the road and pedaled downhill, arriving well after midnight.

"I lay awake almost all night, reliving the pleasure of our evening together, remembering the picnic with the sounds of water still rushing in my ears. I thought of being close to Ian, protected by him. Yes, I could envision a life with him.

"But Ian became distant over the next few days. Finally he told me that he needed to return to Paris.

"I sensed there was something wrong, in spite of his assurances. When I returned to Paris, there was a brief letter waiting for me explaining that he was returning to the United States to go to law school. He told me that he had a great time with me and wanted to come back to Paris and see more of me in the future. He promised he would be in touch, but I didn't hear from him for years."

"More abandonment," nodded Ana as she handed the box of tissues to Emma.

"Yes, that was awful for me. I thought that I had found someone who would start to heal the wounds of my early life. Instead, it only got worse."

"I know this is painful for you, Emma, but I want you to get it all out on the table with me, so we can take a look at it. Tell me what happened next."

"I read and reread his letter trying to understand what had gone wrong, why he had he run away. I felt ripped apart and yes, abandoned again. For almost a week, I wandered in a daze, looking at the river and sitting on its banks, hating Ian and also longing for him.

"On an early autumn afternoon, I stumbled into the Beaux-Arts café and was nursing a Perrier, looking out the window from the smoke-filled room when Marguerite Henri approached my table. She was a well-known broadcast journalist. I had met her at a school art exhibit. We had dinner occasionally. She had shoulder-length straight black hair, olive skin, and sparkling hazel eyes that usually gave off a hard glare, but that day, her expression softened. I must have looked pretty bad.

"'My goodness. Things can't be that bad, dear child,' Marguerite said. She could see that I was pregnant.

"'You must forgive me,' I burst out, embarrassed at the familiarity that was out of character for both of us.

"Marguerite sat next to me and lightly touched my hand.

"'There are only two things that can cause this much distress. Your mother died, or the man who got you pregnant has left you,' she said.

"'My mother is already dead. But you guessed correctly. I was really starting to love him, but he disappeared and went back to his country, leaving me like this,' I stammered, shocked at how it was all coming out.

"The journalist listened, in silence. I found her quiet attentiveness comforting. It opened my heart.

"'Come with me,' she said. 'I will feed you this evening.'"

"It is very moving, what you're telling me, Emma, but our session is over for today. Will you come back tomorrow at the same time?" asked Ana.

"Yes," Emma stammered, "thank you for giving me this outlet, Ana." She got up and hugged Ana, then walked out into the garden past the Walt Whitman wall and made her way to the gate.

10

What Did Maurice Do with the Boy?

SAMUEL WAS BESIDE HIMSELF. He didn't know if he should go to San Francisco and try to get Maurice to cooperate, or if he should stay in Big Sur and try to find Alain. If he couldn't find the boy, perhaps he could at least pick up a clue about where he might have gone, or where Maurice had hidden him. Early the next morning, Samuel got on the phone and talked it over with Sergeant Patruski. Patruski advised him that the evidence collected at the cabins was still being processed. Maurice was still not talking, and he had hired a lawyer. Knowing all this, Samuel called Emma and told her that he would stay in Big Sur and look for Alain with Deputy Sheriff Smathers of the Monterey County Search and Rescue Squad.

Smathers was a big, tall, muscular man. He had a blond crew cut and seldom wore headgear. He worked with a bloodhound that had been trained by the FBI for search and rescue missions before it was sold to the sheriff's department. Samuel, the deputy, and the dog went back to the first cabin. The men checked to see if Alain was hiding nearby, or if had come back to use the cabin to keep warm. Smathers brought out a battery operated megaphone. He asked Samuel to identify himself and call to the boy.

When there wasn't any answer, the deputy led the dog into

the chamber where Alain had been kept. He had the animal jump on the bed and smell the bare mattress. The blankets, sheets, and pillow cases had already been removed and taken to San Francisco. Next he led him to the places where the vomit had dried on the carpet. Once Smathers thought the dog was ready, they went down the forested slope to see if the boy had left a trail, or if there was other evidence that he had escaped. It was a bright day, and the weather was crisp. At first, they thought the dog had picked up Alain's scent, but after an hour of wandering around the area, he seemed lost. It was as though he had been wearing snowshoes.

"Do you think the boy might have been on a sled?" asked Samuel.

"The terrain is too steep for that. I can't figure out what it is," said Smathers.

It was clear that the dog couldn't either, and there was no other evidence that the boy had been on the mountainside near the cabin. They tried letting the dog check the adult footprints around the area to see if he could pick up a scent of the boy being carried back to the cabin. Then they backtracked down the mountainside to the see if the boy had discarded a piece of clothing in his escape. That didn't work either.

After spending the morning searching the mountainside around the first cabin, they went to the second. They repeated the process by giving the dog a piece of the mattress and a piece of carpet where the boy's vomit had been. The dog sniffed around the cabin with no response. Then they went down the mountainside to the area where Maurice had been captured, but it was no use. It was clear to both of them that the dog was clueless.

"I assume you've been doing this for a long time, Mr. Smathers. Does the fact that your dog picked up no scent around here mean that the boy wasn't here?"

"That's what it means to me concerning this cabin. You

saw the dog's first reaction at the other site. He was on the scent until a certain point. It either means that the adult caught the boy and took him back by carrying him so that he didn't touch the ground or that the boy used some device to cover his scent tracks. Did this kid know anything about such things? It's pretty sophisticated."

"I'll find out as soon as I get in touch with his mother. Is there any way to tell if the boy substituted the kidnapper's scent for his own? This boy and his mother are personal friends of mine. I need to find this kid and find him alive. I'm a mess until I do."

"I have watched you since you got here. I can tell it's personal with you, and I want to help as much as I can. I'll give him something that belonged to the kidnapper and let's see where it leads. But we'll have to go back to the first cabin again." He took out a beret that belonged to Maurice and let the dog sniff it. He wandered around the inside of the cabin and then went down the mountainside again to where Maurice had been captured.

They returned to the first cabin, gave him Maurice's beret to sniff again and let the dog loose. He went down the hill to where he had lost the boy's scent and then climbed back up the hill to the cabin. He then went out to where the bus had been parked. The dog stopped there, slobbering, panting and barking. He had nothing more to offer.

It was now the end of daylight. Samuel called Emma from the substation and told her all that had happened that day.

He also asked her if Alain had any training in dog tracking. "Yes," she answered. "He studied the army survival manual, and he talked to me about it several times."

"I remember seeing some survival manuals in his bedroom? Did he read or study them?"

"Yes. He devoured them."

"I have to tell you, Emma, that's our best hope right now,

that he escaped and is living on the land and hiding in the mountains here in Big Sur because he doesn't know that the kidnapper has been captured."

"What about newspaper and radio coverage? Won't that help?"

"I doubt that he has access to either radio or newspapers. He's probably scared out of his wits."

"I have faith in him. He has a special relationship with animals. In many ways, he gets along better with them than with humans."

"Very interesting boy, Emma. I have to come back to San Francisco tonight, but I'll get back down here tomorrow or as soon as I can, and I will keep looking until I find him, I promise you."

Samuel passed on this information to Smathers, then called Bernardi to tell him what he had learned, and to advise him that he was on his way back to San Francisco.

* * *

When Samuel was back in Bernardi's office the next morning, he described his total inability to track Alain's path.

Bernardi told him about Maurice's refusal to cooperate and his request for a lawyer who spoke French. He had asked to contact the French consul for help, and the consul came up with one who agreed to represent him. The lawyer was Michel DeLuc, a well-known and respected member of the criminal bar of San Francisco attorneys.

"That name sounds familiar to me," said Samuel. "When I was in Paris, I saw a sign for the Luc DeLuc detective agency. I wonder if there's any connection?"

"I guess we'll find out," said Bernardi. "I set up a meeting with him and his client this morning. I'll hide you in the backroom with the two-way mirror."

Later that morning Bernardi, Seargeant Patruski, and an assistant district attorney sat on one side of the table, with their backs to the mirror, while the lawyer, Michel DeLuc, sat on the other side giving Samuel a good view of him. DeLuc was above average height with a full head of brown hair combed straight back. He had piercing blue eyes and a strong jaw. If he hadn't chosen law he could have passed for a movie actor. He wore a double-breasted gray suit that was perfectly tailored and looked expensive.

Samuel wondered how Maurice could afford such high-priced legal talent. He was escorted to the room by a deputy sheriff handcuffed to a leather belt around his waist and shackled at the ankles with leg irons. He looked haggard and depressed. He was placed next to his lawyer and they acknowledged each other with a few words spoken in French. Maurice looked listless and sad; his face was drawn, and even his beard looked disheveled.

As soon as all were seated, DeLuc took charge. "Gentlemen," he said with his suave French accent. "My client acknowledges that he took the child, even though he disputes the charge of kidnapping. We are prepared to cut a deal as long as his right to appeal is preserved on his claim of paternity."

"That's not his only problem, Mr. DeLuc," said Bernardi.

"What are you trying to say?"

"Two young boys were murdered, and a third one is missing. Put that in the pot, and it doesn't look too good for your client."

"Wait a minute. He took his son, he admits that. The rest is a nonstarter. That has nothing to do with Mr. Levantine."

"I'm advising you of what's out there and unaccounted for. Now, your client has a chance to do right by himself and give us the last boy he took," said Bernardi.

Patruski lifted his arm and moved his lips as if he were going to say something, but nothing came out. He put his arm down.

"What I'm trying to tell you is that Mr. Levantine doesn't know where the boy is. He escaped."

Patruski scowled. "Come on, DeLuc. That's the biggest and oldest bullshit story in the book. As of right now, all the deaths point to your client."

"Hold on, Sergeant. I came here to see if I could help you, not so you could abuse my client. I've already admitted to you that he took Alain. The question remains if he was entitled to. He claims the boy was his son, and that raises redeeming circumstances. The rest of your claims are not worth talking about; and therefore, we refuse to go on with them. I assure you, you have the wrong man. I'm going to say it again, the boy escaped." He squinted his eyes and looked intently at Patruski. "We'll see you in court."

"When we find the body, your client is going to the gas chamber," said Patruski as he slouched back in the chair with a disgusted look on his face.

DeLuc stood up. "Please remove the prisoner, sir," he said looking at the deputies.

Patruski pointed to the prisoner. "Get him out of here."

Two deputies came forward, one on each side of Levantine, lifted him out of his seated position, and escorted him out of the room. He looked worse than when he came into the room.

Samuel, watching from behind the two-way mirror, waited for Maurice to leave and clear the hallway, then he went to the door of the interrogation room where the deputy let him in. Patruski and Bernardi were having a heated argument

"I didn't like you threatening him with the gas chamber," said Bernardi.

"The son of a bitch pissed me off. How many times have you heard that line, Lieutenant? The story that the victim escaped usually comes from a guilty bastard. You've been around long enough to know that. Come on."

Samuel, red faced, interrupted the argument. "I believe Levantine. The kid knows about outdoor survival. I think he's out there. The only question is how do we find him."

"I hope you're right for the boy's sake and for his mother's as well. But I can't take any more of this shit," said Patruski, and he got up and left.

Samuel and Bernardi looked at each other. Samuel shook his head. "I'm worried about the safety of the boy. I need to see if DeLuc can get Maurice to give us any more information. I'm going to his office when I leave here."

"Do you think he'll talk with you?"

"I hope so. If Levantine helps us, he'll also be saving himself. I'll talk to you this afternoon."

* * *

Samuel went to the phone booth in the basement of the Hall of Justice, made a call to Emma, and told her what had transpired. He assured her that he thought the boy was alive and hiding in the wilderness of Big Sur. He bought a cup of coffee, reviewed his notes, and then called DeLuc's office.

When the lawyer got on the phone he identified himself as Samuel Hamilton, a reporter from the afternoon newspaper and a friend of Emma, the boy's mother.

"I know who you are. You're also a sidekick of the head of homicide. Why should I talk with you?"

"Because I believe you. Your client didn't kill anyone. He took the boy, and the boy escaped. I know that. I went to the cabin and saw for myself. I just need to know more about how he escaped. Can I come to your office and talk this over with you?"

"All right. But make it snappy. I'm still not sure about you, Mr. Hamilton."

"I can help you defend your client, if you let me."

85

Samuel took the bus to Kearny Street, walked down to Montgomery, entered the Russ Building, and rode up to the sixteenth floor. He entered a smartly furnished office with expensive art on the walls. He sat on one of the fancy chairs and was served a cup of coffee. In a few minutes, DeLuc came to the reception area to retrieve him and took him back to an elegant office overlooking the Bay. "Have a seat, Mr. Hamilton. As I told you, I haven't made up my mind about you."

"Listen, Mr. DeLuc. I know the boy. I know his mother, and I knew his father."

"The boy's alleged father, you mean."

"All right, alleged. I spoke with Alain's mother. He's studied survival in the wilderness. I just need to know how he avoided the dog tracking his scent."

DeLuc was quiet while Samuel talked, and he remained so when he stopped. The reporter was about to comment about the silence when the lawyer spoke up.

"All right. I'm going to tell you what Mr. Levantine told me about the boy, but I want it off the record. I realize you may testify to all this if forced to. This is a highly unusual situation. I've never been in this position before in all my years of practice, but I believe that you want to help my client. There was a bear rug in the room where the boy was hidden. He took it with him and slid down the mountainside. If the dog lost the boy's scent, as you say he did, it was probably because he confused it with the bear's."

"That may explain it. It looked like he was on a sled or something similar. It could have been the bear rug. I was with the dog and his handler, so it makes sense to me."

"I'm going to tell you something else in confidence. My client was relieved when the boy escaped. He noticed that Alain was strange, maybe even retarded. So he was happy not to have to deal with him any more. He hadn't bargained for that kind of behavior. It didn't fit his fantasy of connecting with a long-lost son."

Samuel reacted with outrage, but he bit his lip. DeLuc went on, "What's with the Lieutenant implying that my client might be involved in the murders of those two boys?"

"That was just Patruski ranting. There aren't any leads, so, of course, he'd like to pin them on your client."

11

Melba Figures Out a Way to Help

SAMUEL CALLED EMMA from a pay phone on Montgomery Street to let her know he was on his way there. Reyna received him and offered him a hot cup of tea and an Algerian pastry. He explained to them both what he'd learned from DeLuc about the bear rug. He also shared the comment that Maurice was relieved at the escape because he found the boy's behavior strange.

Emma grimaced at Maurice's description of her son. "He's not strange, Samuel. He's unique. He is a very solitary and sensitive boy with intellectual interests way beyond his years. That's why he studies all these esoteric things."

"Why would he think that he was retarded?" asked Reyna.

"Precisely because he lives in his own world. Why would he share his secrets with his kidnapper?" Emma added.

"I remember your telling me that he had a special affinity with animals. What kind of animals?"

"All kinds. He spends a lot of time alone at the zoo conversing and connecting with wild animals."

"For instance?"

"I mean the man-eating kind. He feels comfortable with them."

"I guess that has to be good news, if that's the right way to put it, since he's out in the wilderness with bears, coyotes, and mountain lions."

"Samuel, I'm worried sick about my son, but I can't go to the mountains and look for him myself."

"You go and get support from Ana. I'm working on a plan right now, but I have to get the details straight in my head before I take the next step. We'll talk tomorrow."

* * *

Emma rang the bell at the *vesica piscis* gate. She waited for Ana to buzz her through, walked past the Walt Whitman quote, and into the herb garden where Merlin stood guard. Ana was waiting for her by her consultation room. She entered and sat in the rocking chair.

"Tell me, Emma, what are you feeling?"

"Sad and worried sick because they haven't found my son, but I am encouraged. Samuel told me that he escaped. I know that Alain is alive. He has been studying the outdoors from the time he was a young boy, but that doesn't help my anxiety."

"Did the kidnapper hurt him?"

"He says not. He claimed that he is his father, and that's why he took him."

"Is that possible?"

"Not at all. Several months passed between the last time I was with him and when I met Ian, the boy's father. I was already in the fall semester of my first year at Beaux-Arts. I last had anything to do with Maurice in the early summer."

"He must be a lonely and desperate man."

Emma looked hard at Ana. "He is a bastard. He stole my child. Then after spending just a few days with Alain, he decided the boy was retarded and wanted to get rid of him."

"Don't you think that helped him in his escape?"

"What do you mean?"

"Since he thought his behavior was so strange, he didn't make a thorough search for him."

Emma laughed sarcastically. "I doubt that. Alain just outsmarted him. He slid down the mountainside on a bear rug so he couldn't be traced. That part I understand and am proud of him for that. I'm sure that Maurice was relieved because the boy was much more than he bargained for. But the fact that Alain disappeared worries me, even though he knows what he's doing in the wilderness. It certainly doesn't change Maurice's responsibility for putting him in so much potential danger."

"Has the boy had other experiences like that?"

"That's almost the right question to ask. His knowledge comes from books. It really depends on how he applies what he's learned from what he's studied."

"Will Samuel help you find him?"

"Samuel has been a good friend and a rock through all this. He brought me to you. I really don't know what I would do without him."

"Are you angry with him for causing your accident?"

Emma rocked back and forth a few times in her chair, looking directly at the Goddess of Mercy. "After the accident happened, I was very angry at him. He came to see me in the hospital, and at first I wouldn't talk to him. After he showed up every day for a week, I changed my mind. I realized that my personal problems were much bigger than what he did to me. Since then, he's been a very good friend, and he has helped me both financially and emotionally, especially when Ian was killed in Vietnam. It's like having an uncle who doesn't have any money but a big heart."

Ana smiled. "That's a very generous observation. It shows what kind of a person you are. The last time you were here, you started to tell me about Marguerite Henri. Do you want to go on?"

Emma paused for a moment as she reminisced. "She was the daughter of a French military officer and a wealthy Algerian socialite named Reyna. She lived in Algeria until the age of twenty. When the rebels assassinated her father, she and her mother fled the country. They settled in Paris in a spacious apartment on the Quai des Grand Augustins. You remember, she came over to me in the café, and I was very distraught. She took me to her apartment. It was modestly decorated but overlooked the river and was full of light. It had three large bedrooms, a spacious living room and kitchen, and a very interesting bathroom with a Roman tub that the previous owner, an Iranian businessman with extravagant taste, had installed. He also expanded the ceiling heights, which made the apartment appear much roomier that it actually was.

"Her mother was a plump and very affectionate woman in her mid-fifties. I attached myself to her immediately."

"Sounds like it was a nice place where they lived."

"When I walked into their living room I was in pieces. I was pregnant, felt abandoned, and was suffering from morning sickness. I tried to control myself and almost succeeded until Reyna sat beside me on the sofa and started stroking my trembling shoulders. Then I broke down in uncontrollable tears. While her mother tried to console me, Marguerite went to the bathroom and drew warm water into the tub. She beckoned me to the bathroom while she poured aromatic oils into the bath."

"'Come and get in. It will soothe and calm you like nothing else in the world,' she offered.

"She helped me disrobe and guided me into the tub, while Reyna softly made fun of me for being embarrassed in front of only women. Then they began to plaster me with mud from the banks of the Chéliff River in Algeria, which they used to bathe their own sorrows away. My resistance disappeared. I had never had such an intimate experience before. I felt the tension drain from my body, soothed by a gentleness that I had never known, even as a child. I sighed with great relief, profoundly grateful to these strangers who extended their kindness without question or fuss."

"Why are you going into this detail with me, Emma?"

"I want you to understand how lonely and desperate I was and how those women surrounded me with affection.

"After my bath, Reyna served a meal of lamb stew laden with cumin on a bed of couscous and a fresh salad of cucumbers and tomatoes and, of course, more Arabic mint tea.

"I left their apartment well after nine o'clock, feeling like another person, relaxed and refreshed. I was still emotional, but I felt I would be able to live with it."

"I imagine there is a big difference from the way you feel now?"

Emma started to cry slowly. "Yes, I felt loved and supported. Now I still have Reyna and Samuel to hold on to, but Samuel doesn't belong to me. And the person I love most is in danger, and I can do nothing, and no one can assuage the pain."

"That's what we're here to talk about, your feelings. Continue."

"Marguerite and I met often in the ensuing weeks. One Sunday in early November when it was blustering outside, Marguerite cautioned me not to stuff myself with junk food. She told me I needed protein and fresh vegetables, and I needed to keep my weight in check.

"I told her that her mother kept sending me all these sweets. They were impossible to refuse. She was so kind!"

Emma was smiling now. "She said she would have to talk with her mother, that she was always trying to spoil everybody with sweets, the Algerian way. Then she said this astonishing thing. She told me that she and her mother had been discussing me since she brought me home that day. And since I was growing large and having to climb four flights of stairs several time a day, they wanted me to come and live with them until the baby was born. She said they had an extra room that filled with sunshine, and it would be perfect for me, and to reach their flat I would only have to climb one flight of stairs.

"I was so surprised and moved that it took me several minutes to find my voice. I told her that she was so generous and caring! But I needed to think about it. I asked if I could let her know in a couple of days. I asked her what I would do with my cat, Charbon. He had been such a good companion to me."

"She said, 'Don't worry about Charbon. We have mice that need to be taken care of, and I am sure he was made for the job.'

"Even though I asked for time to think about it, I knew immediately that was the place for me. I could not turn down so much affection and support. Besides, I was not ready to tell my father that I was pregnant. I knew he would disown me.

"What had started out as a nightmare took an unexpected turn. These two extraordinary women were offering the affection and protection that Ian had refused me. I put my hands on my hard belly and smiled for the first time since I realized that I was pregnant. We are safe, little one, I murmured to my baby, thinking of my own mother."

"What about your father, Emma? Where was he, while all this was going on?"

"When I finally did muster the courage to tell him that I was pregnant, and not married, he slammed down the phone and didn't talk to me for a long time. Not until after Alain was born. And up to that moment he was my closest connection. When the phone went dead, I felt that I had lost my right arm."

* * *

93

Samuel was sitting with Bernardi at the Round Table at Camelot. The lieutenant was drinking dago red while Samuel jiggled the ice in his scotch and Melba took a drag on her Lucky Strike and sipped her bottle of Schlitz beer. Excalibur had already gobbled his treat and was sleeping at Melba's feet under the table.

Samuel had been in earlier and had brought her up to date on what had happened in Big Sur.

Bernardi looked worried. "I'm getting a lot of heat from the chief and from the families of the two murdered boys. They want me to get moving on the investigation, so I'm not sure what to do in Big Sur except to bring in a team from the FBI."

"It sounds to me like finding that boy is a job for Excalibur," Melba said.

The three looked at each other quizzically and laughed.

"You know that's not so farfetched," said Samuel, standing up. "Remember that this one-eared and tailless ugly dog led us to O'Hara's apartment through the tunnels of Chinatown, and that helped solve the murder case of the Chinese Jars."

"You mean he's better than a bloodhound?" said Bernardi.

"Much better. But we can't wait too long to get him down there because those scents dissipate."

"Well, get started," insisted Melba. "Stay with me for awhile, Samuel, and I'll teach you how to feed him and make sure he doesn't catch cold at night. He'll be excited to go on a vacation with you."

Bernardi excused himself. "I have to leave. If you take charge of this, I'll put a couple of men on the murder cases and see if we can make some progress."

"As soon as I find the boy, I'll get on those cases with you," said Samuel.

"Your only job right now is to see if you can find the boy. Don't clutter your head with anything else."

Samuel looked at him and at Melba and shrugged his shoulders. Melba took a drag on her Lucky Strike and nodded approvingly. She could tell that Samuel felt the weight of the job with his entire being.

Bernardi finished his glass of wine and left Camelot.

When he was gone, Samuel sat back down with Melba.

"Don't you want to come with me and take care of Excalibur?"

"Not a chance in hell. I'm in such bad shape, I'd catch pneumonia and kick the bucket. Then you'd have to take care of him full time. Now, wouldn't you just love that?"

"I see your point. Can we leave tomorrow? Does that give us enough time?"

"Sure, you pick him up at my house at ten. I'll have his food prepared for a week. Make sure you feed him twice a day, I'll give you a sweater to keep him warm. Make sure he uses it. He's not young anymore."

"I have to call Marcel and see if he can go with me. I'll be right back." He walked to the rear of the bar, called the photographer, and discussed the situation with him, explaining that they were going to search for the missing boy in Big Sur and could be gone for as much as a week. Marcel said he had to clear his calendar and would call back. Samuel gave him the phone number of the bar and went back to the Round Table to get as much information as he could from Melba. He also called Officer Smathers to make arrangements to meet him and to borrow equipment for the search.

12

Will They Find a Pot of Gold at the End of the Rainbow or a Dead Body?

Samuel and Marcel with Excalibur in the back seat arrived in Big Sur and went to a motel that allowed pets. As planned, the deputy showed up at seven o'clock. The trio had breakfast at a café on Highway One. The deputy was dressed in fatigues and combat boots. Samuel and Marcel both had on Pendleton plaid shirts, Levis, and tennis shoes—a professional law enforcement officer dressed for the job and two misfits who looked more like a couple of vagrants he'd picked up hitchhiking.

"You told me that you were in the army before you joined the sheriff's office."

"Yes, sir. From just after the Korean War until last year. The only reason why I got out was because Southeast Asia was heating up and from the stories the vets told me, war is the shits, especially for an infantryman such as myself."

"That's what I wanted to talk to you about. You were a captain in charge of a company, right?"

"Yes, sir."

"Would you plan the strategy to attack and to defend terrain?"

"That was my job, and me and my staff spent a lot of time

with battalion intelligence studying just that."

"I read once that the idea is to protect the high ground. You defend it if it's yours, or you attack to get it," said Samuel. "My point is that this young man knows a lot about strategy."

"Are you kidding? He's just an eleven-year-old boy."

"A very exceptional one. Since he's studied survival, we can bet he's also studied sticking to the high ground so he can escape down the back side of a mountain if he sees the enemy coming, and let's face it, everyone is the enemy to him."

"Is there something wrong with this kid?"

"Let's just say he's unusual," said Samuel.

The three went out to the parking lot. "I think we should only take my van," said the deputy.

"You'll have to follow us to our motel so we can leave my car there," said Marcel.

They met at the motel and all piled into the deputy's vehicle. Excalibur and the bloodhound sniffed each other in all the usual places and relaxed. "What's the dog's name?" asked Samuel.

"Snoop. What's yours?"

"Excalibur," said Samuel.

Samuel had spent what remained of the afternoon the day before with Sergeant Patruski discussing the case and looking over the evidence that Patruski's team had collected at the cabin site. Samuel asked Patruski if he wanted to be part of the search team, but he begged off, saying that he would chase down leads in San Francisco while Samuel was away.

They chose articles of the boy's clothing and some of the other vomit-stained rug for the dog to sniff. They put them in a sealed container until needed, so they would remain as uncontaminated as possible from other scents. They planned to take them out one by one, so as to preserve their odors' strength.

Samuel also borrowed three sets of binoculars so he, Marcel, and Deputy Smathers could scour the mountainsides. It turned out that Smathers had his own special binoculars that he'd kept when he left the army.

The three men and the two dogs stared at the cabin from which the boy had escaped. When they reached it, Samuel opened the container and allowed both dogs to sniff the saturated piece of rug he'd brought from San Francisco.

"Let's start at the part of the slope where it looks like Alain was sliding on the bear rug," said Samuel. They led the dogs down to the spot and unleashed them. The dogs ran wildly around the area, sniffing and barking, but soon Excalibur came back to Samuel and put his paws on his waist in anticipation of a treat. Samuel gave him one and made sure Snoop also had his, with the permission of Smathers.

"What now?" said Smathers.

"Let's go down, and as we're climbing back up towards the top on the other side, we'll unleash them again and see if they pick up something."

Samuel called out to Alain on the megaphone and asked him to contact them. They leashed the dogs and the dogs pulled them down the slope for forty-five minutes until they reached the valley floor. Samuel again let the dogs sniff the piece of rug and then released them. For several minutes both dogs rushed along yelping next to the stream bed that flowed down the valley toward the sea. Then they headed up another mountainside. Samuel had been through this sort of search with Excalibur in the tunnels of San Francisco's Chinatown, so he knew to just let the dog have his way. Marcel recorded the trip with a Leica thirty-five millimeter point and shoot camera with an extra sensitive fifty millimeter 1.4 lens.

"They're on to something," said Samuel as they watched both dogs moving rapidly up the steep incline. He again called out to Alain over the megaphone. "Do you think we can keep up with them?"

"It would be worse for us if we had to control them," said

Smathers. "We'd die of exhaustion."

"They won't get lost, will they?" asked Marcel.

"Not a chance," said both Samuel and Smathers at the same time. "They know what they're doing," said Smathers. "Listen to them. Just keep moving and drink plenty of water."

"Snoop sure does slobber a lot," said Samuel.

"I guess you've never seen a bloodhound in action," laughed Smathers.

Samuel and Marcel laughed. "Yeah, I'm used to Excalibur, he's much quieter about what he's doing."

"Doesn't matter, if he gets the same results," said Smathers.

The climb to the top took more than an hour and a half. The dogs were way ahead of them, but they kept yelping so they were easy to locate. Samuel called to them to heel. Excalibur came immediately, and Snoop hesitatingly followed him. It paid off. Samuel gave each another treat, and they hooked leashes up to the harnesses. All three men were out of breath, but Samuel and Marcel were far more spent than the fit Smathers.

"They're definitely on to something connected to the boy," said Smathers. "It's amazing. Excalibur was the key here. He gave Snoop extra energy."

"It's one of the mysteries of life," said Samuel. They all laughed. "While we're up here on top and trying to catch our breath, let's talk about military strategy."

Smathers took out a map that he'd rolled up in a cylinder. He spread it on the ground and held it open in place with four rocks. He explained the contour lines to Samuel and Marcel and showed them where they were on it. "We have to move over here to the edge of the high ground and take a look."

"How far away are we from this place you're pointing to?" asked Samuel.

"I'd say about a hundred yards that way," said Smathers,

and he took out his binoculars and searched the foreground and pointed to the edge of the flat ground in the distance.

Samuel and Marcel also took out their binoculars and looked at the terrain. Then they all walked with the dogs to the designated area.

"This is the high ground," said Smathers. "From here he can see the enemy coming from all sides."

"Does that mean that Alain, if he were up here, could see us coming?" asked Samuel.

The dogs were on leash but were barking and straining to get free, and Snoop continued to slobber.

"Let's look around and see if any of the area has been disturbed. That way we can tell if he's been here," said Smathers, "but from the way the dogs are acting they're picking up his scent." There were tall pine trees with needles covering the ground, and the breeze was still coming from the ocean. The smell of salt was in the air. There were several rocks jutting out of the mountainside. From where they were, it looked as if nothing had been disturbed.

They kept searching different parts of the area for evidence Alain had been there. "Here's something that looks like there was a fire, but it's not enough to be sure," said Samuel.

The dogs acted otherwise, as they both yelped and strained even harder to get free. They obviously had picked up the boy's scent.

"Whoever cleaned this up was a real pro," said Smathers, above the barking dogs, "and if you look closely, you can see that there were several fires. We're on the right track, look at the dogs struggling to get free."

"Should we let 'em go?" asked Samuel.

"No, no. We don't want Alain to run for it. Let's keep them harnessed until we see him." He again announced his presence to Alain over the megaphone.

In the meantime Marcel was snapping photos of what

had apparently been the fire pit. The dogs were restless and pulling them toward one side of the mountain top.

"What are we looking for?" asked Samuel.

"For a place he could hide and sleep safely at night, a hollowed out tree trunk that's still standing, or a cave, something like that."

They all used their binoculars and scoured the area slightly down slope on the other side of the point where they had been standing. None of them could detect any sign of a hiding place.

"Let's follow the dogs. We're pretty close to this young man," said Smathers.

"Are you sure he can hear them barking from where he's hiding?" said Samuel.

"Positive, I'm just waiting for him to move because of it, so we can see him," said Smathers.

They started their pursuit down slope as the dogs led the way, straining at their harnesses and yelping loudly. It was a welcome relief for Samuel and Marcel to be walking downhill for a change. Samuel was being pulled rapidly by Excalibur, but his descent was uneven because it required balance, and that didn't come easy to him. Marcel had to stumble along, a captive of the dogs as well. Smathers, on the other hand, was in his element. He strode along confidently as if he did this every day.

They all scoured the terrain. Smathers brought them to a halt. "We're pretty close to him."

"No kidding," said Samuel, pulling the leash hard to stop Excalibur's charge. "He's on to the boy's scent. It's going to be difficult from here on for me to hold him." He took off his hat with one hand and wiped the sweat off his forehead with his forearm.

"Look down there," said Smathers. "There's a huge redwood stump. On the other side we may find a hiding place. I can let Snoop loose and he can charge into it."

"No, don't do that," said Samuel. "Let's split them up. You go on one side with Snoop, and I'll go on the other with Excalibur. That way, if he tries to run, one of them will find him."

"We can try, but since both dogs are following the same scent, I doubt we can separate them."

Smathers was correct; the dogs wouldn't separate. Samuel motioned to Marcel to move towards the left side while he and Smathers were dragged to the right by the barking dogs.

The three men and the two dogs were looking down slope. The dogs were pulling on their harnesses and the sun was directly overhead. They started down with the dogs in the lead with Samuel and Smathers being dragged behind. The dogs were heading towards the large tree stump at least eight feet high and bigger than that in diameter. When they arrived and went around the base, they saw a hollowed-out cave which provided protection from the elements. The dogs wanted to keep going but Samuel held them up.

"Look inside. There's the bear rug." He went in and poked around and finally found some dried plants and berries neatly concealed in the dirt and in the walls that he surmised must have been used for food. "The boy obviously made this his hideout. What do you make of it, Mr. Smathers?"

"Pretty clever kid," he yelled, over the barking dogs. "If you look at these tracks, he spends a lot of time here. Obviously, this is where he sleeps."

"The question is, where is he right now?" asked Samuel, while Marcel was snapping photos, documenting the find.

"I wouldn't be surprised if he moved out of here in a hurry when he heard us coming. He's probably watching us from a distance."

"Up or down?" said Samuel. "These dogs are giving me a headache."

"My guess is both up and down because that's what I would do if someone were chasing me. But the dogs will show us which way he went. I think one of us should stay here, while the other searches. You should be the one to go after him because he knows you, and if he sees me or my dog, he'll only get scared and keep running," said Smathers.

"I don't think that's a good idea," said Samuel. "If I chase him and he comes back here and finds you, he'll just keep running. Let's let the dogs get a good whiff and all of us keep going."

Excalibur and Snoop rummaged around the bear rug and the hidden firewood and stash of food. Then they went outside, both still yelping, and headed up the hill pulling Samuel and Smathers behind them. It was in another direction from that which they'd come and not down slope where they'd been heading.

"I'm glad you're with us, Mr. Smathers. I would have thought he ran down the mountain. He could move faster."

"I get you," said Smathers. "The dogs have got the scent. That's all we need. I don't think he's too far away and I'm sure he's watching us."

Samuel again blasted his message from the battery operated megaphone, asking Alain not to move. The three started the slow steady climb back up the mountain led by Excalibur, barking and straining at his harness. It was clear he knew exactly where he wanted to go. He stopped beside a large boulder that protruded several feet off the ground and sniffed at the trampled pine needles at the base.

"It's obvious he climbed this rock to watch us," said Samuel. "I wonder if he has binoculars." He scanned up and down the slope and finally fixed on the cave, some hundred yards away.

Sizing up the situation, Samuel whispered something to Smathers and Marcel, and then he released Excalibur, who headed straight for the cave with Samuel running after him, quite out of breath. When he got there he saw Excalibur, yelping and licking the face of Alain who was again hiding under the bear rug. "Alain, it's Samuel. We're so happy to find you safe," he said, tears streaming down his cheeks.

Right behind Samuel was Marcel with a big smile on his face snapping photos. Alain pushed the bear rug down from his face, smiling too.

"Do you recognize me, Alain? It's Samuel," he said, wiping the tears from his face.

Alain's face slowly changed from a smile to serious, but he said nothing.

"Looking for you has been one of the most painful experiences of my life. Finding you safe is one of the most wonderful things that has ever happened to me."

The boy broke his silence. "I heard the dogs from a long way off, but I wasn't sure if Maurice was after me or the police, so I started running as fast as I could, and I tried to stay hidden. Then I heard you on the loud speaker, so I stopped running because I knew it was you. I'm glad it was you and not Maurice. I am very proud of my escape and how I fooled that nut."

He was caked with dirt, but his smile was back. His clothes smelled, and he looked tired but healthy. All good signs, thought Samuel, considering the ordeal he'd been through over the last two weeks.

Samuel flashed over all of the events since he'd heard of Alain's kidnapping, but he set them aside for the moment. What was important to him now was to get him to a doctor to check out his health and then to get the child reunited with his mother and grandmother. Smathers and Snoop were in the background, watching. Excalibur sat by the boy's side, licking him and standing guard. Alain responded by hugging Excalibur with obvious relief.

Part 2

13

Digging Deeper

THERE WERE NOW TWO dramas unfolding in Samuel's world—helping Emma and Alain deal with the ordeal they that had been through and focusing on the homicides of the two young boys. He had put the murders aside until Alain was found and brought safely home. Since Emma had the help of Reyna and Ana Cejas for the time being, he started delving into the evidence that related to the two deaths.

His first conversation was with Bernardi in his office overlooking the freeway. "Good work finding the boy," Bernardi said. "I know it's a great relief to you, and I can't even imagine what it means to his mother."

"I couldn't think of anything else until it was done," said Samuel.

"And it's a relief not to have another murder on our hands."

"Which brings up another problem," said Samuel. "Patruski and the DA want to prosecute Maurice for murder as well as kidnapping, but it's my position that he didn't kill those two boys. If you're with them on that theory, then you and I have a conflict."

"I really don't know yet. Right now, they're still cases in progress, so I'm in charge of the investigation. I'll hold them off as long as I can. Take a look at the file. If you want to use Mac, he's available. While this isn't official, it's our deal, and I'll stick to it. Frankly we don't know any more than we did before Alain went missing, except that the two murdered boys were sexually molested."

Samuel reviewed the file, then contacted Mac and asked him if would accompany him to the alleyway south of Market. He wanted to expand the search for clues prior to Alain's kidnapping.

Mac and Samuel drove in the crime scene van to the alley where the boys had been murdered. Mac placed the van at the entrance to the alley so no one would interfere with their search. It was midday and the sun was directly overhead. Nevertheless, Mac took out a pair of flashlights and handed one to Samuel. They both walked to the brick wall at the end of the alley. Full garbage cans lined the alley on both sides spewing trash that had not been picked up yet. Samuel shuddered as they looked at the blood spatters from the killings that had taken place there.

"Look," said Samuel, "there are pit marks on the wall, and see those pieces of metal stuck in some of them? That must be part of the bullet that passed through one of the boy's head."

"That's a pretty good guess," said Mac, and he started making estimates about where the fragments may have landed. It didn't take long before they found several additional pieces of lead that had ricocheted off the bricks. In all, they quickly located ten pieces of different sizes spread around the scene. They placed them in a plastic bag.

"I wonder why they didn't pick these up when they were out here the first time?" said Samuel.

"Beats me," said Mac. "That really pisses me off. Let's just say it depends on who is doing the looking. I'll try to put this bullet back together at the lab."

"Let's go out another few feet and see if we find any more

pieces," said Samuel.

They moved in unison, backing away from the wall and shining their flashlights on the pavement and to the sides of the alley. Sure enough, they found more fragments, which they also put in the plastic bag.

After they had been doing this for an hour, Mac said, "I think we've got about as much as we're going to get here."

Samuel was uncomfortable, wondering if there was something more that he might have missed. "Let's keep looking for another few minutes, Mac. By the way, there was a black stain on a pant leg of one of the boys. Can you take a look at it? It didn't seem to fit with anything else, and I'd like to know where it came from, if you can tell."

They returned to the brick wall and started back up the alley, probing with their flashlights. Samuel saw something in the shadows of a garbage can, pointed his light at it, and called Mac. They both looked down at the object.

"It looks like an old pile of shit," Mac said.

"Yeah. It sure does, but it doesn't look like the animal kind. It looks human, and it's dried up," said Samuel.

"You want me to pick that up and mark it as evidence? I'm doing this to humor you, you understand," said Mac.

"Yep. I know. But since we're here, we might as well look at everything."

"I'm not complaining. It's just that now I've seen everything."

Samuel turned his light to the other side of the alleyway. "Look, here's another pile that looks even more dried out than that one, and it has a tire imprint running through it."

"Some bum must use this place as a toilet," said Mac. "First I have to get a print of the tire track, and then I have to scrape up the piece of crap." But in spite of his grumbling, he went to work making the mold with his bag of plaster of Paris. After it hardened, he took the imprint off the squashed pile and put it in a bag. Then he scraped up the imprint and put it in another bag and marked both of them.

"I'm not saying they mean anything," said Samuel. "I'm just being thorough."

"Never had a turd solve a murder," said Mac. They both laughed. Samuel helped Mac pack up his evidence box, and they left the alley.

"Can you do me a favor?" asked Samuel. "Will you check and see if the tire print belongs to a police car?"

"You think they all use the same kind of tires?"

"Let's start with that," said Samuel.

They returned to the Hall of Justice, and Samuel went up to Bernardi's office. He found him at his desk. His jacket was hung from a peg on his coat rack, and he was thumbing through a stack of files. "What did you find?" he asked.

Samuel explained the search findings and what Mac was going to do with the fragments of lead and the piles of human excrement that were found at the scene, as well as the imprint of the tire. "He'll be back to us in a few days with his results."

"What can he find out from that?"

"Whether it's human, and if it is, what the person ate. It may be important."

Bernardi thought for a moment. "You never know in this business. Let's look into this a little bit more."

"The crap and the tire track are all long shots," said Samuel.

"Not if we can connect them to the crime. I'll have Mac see if he can find out what kind of car the tire marks came from."

"I've already got him on that," said Samuel. "I'll check with him next week to see what he's come up with. I think it's time to interview the parents, the teachers at the school, and some of the fellow students. Let's see if they can help us shed some light on the killings of those two boys."

Bernardi nodded. "Take a look at the statements that were

taken soon after the crimes were committed, and see what you make of them." He handed Samuel the file.

Samuel browsed through them briefly. "These are pretty perfunctory. Obviously they were in shock because of the recent deaths of the children. Give them a call and see if they will talk to me, and I'll go through them one by one. I see here that Patruski's son knew both boys since they all went to the same school."

"Yeah. He said his son took it pretty hard because they all palled around together. Maybe you should start with Patruski and his son, since they're both within our immediate reach."

"I'd rather wait to interview them because they're easily available to us. They can fill in what I don't get from the others. Can you call the school and let them know I want to interview the teachers and some of the friends other than Patruski's kid? Actually, it's better if I interview the boys at their homes so I get to them one at a time. Let's wait on the interviews with the teachers at school."

* * *

At the same time that Samuel was pursuing leads on the murdered boys, Emma took Alain to meet Ana and have a session with her. They rang the bell. When Ana opened the gate, they strolled through her garden and passed the Walt Whitman quote, the small swimming pool, and the ever vigilant Merlin standing guard. Ana offered each of them a rocking chair, and they sat down next to the bronze statue of Quan Yin, the Goddess of Mercy with her outstretched arms.

"Ana, I want you to meet Alain," Emma said with a joyful smile.

"Hello, Alain, my name is Ana Cejas. I've been talking with your mother over the last few weeks, and I've heard a lot about you. Now I'm very happy to meet you in person and talk with you."

"Thank you, Madam," he said in a noncommittal tone as he looked around at the artifacts in the room. "Is that a statue of a lady?"

"Yes. She is a Chinese goddess who symbolizes the goodness of man's intentions—mercy. She comes from Buddhism. Originally the figure was a man, and then as time went on he was converted to a woman in the Chinese culture. One thing you might really be interested in is that she is also the guardian of animals. I know you are keen on them too.

"Would you mind waiting in the garden, Alain? I have a couple of things to talk to your mother about."

"Sure, I wanted to look around anyway." He walked outside.

"What a lovely child, Emma. You are indeed blessed."

"Now you may see why he is so important to me," she said, blushing.

"He suffered acutely from what happened to him. With your permission, I'd like to see him alone, and see if we can get him through this ordeal."

"I would love for you to, but I am a person of limited means."

"Yes, I know that. We will make adjustments, don't worry. Rather than make him wait in the garden and wonder why we excluded him, will you come back this afternoon by yourself? We will schedule him separately."

"Okay, and thank you for all your help."

"You're welcome, Emma." Ana embraced her, then walked out into the garden to say goodbye to Alain, who was studying the writing on the wall.

"This is a wonderful saying," he said. "I'm looking forward to talking with you about it." Emma came up behind them and grabbed Alain's hand, and they walked out of the garden together.

* * *

Emma came back alone in the afternoon and sat with Ana.

"How are you feeling about Alain's safe return to you?"

"I am overjoyed and, at the same time, scared beyond imagination. I almost can't let him out of my sight. His return is a blessing to me. It's as if I don't deserve it," she said in a worried tone.

Ana nodded. "Tell me more about those feelings."

"So many bad things have happened to me in my life that I secretly didn't believe he would be found alive. At the same time, if he was hurt or killed, it would have destroyed me."

"What are you thinking about right now?"

"I was thinking of when he was born."

"When was that, Emma?"

"That was on May 11, 1953. I was lying in bed with Marguerite, and I felt like I had swallowed a lead balloon. I couldn't have gotten out of bed by myself even if I'd wanted to. I told her something strange was happening to me. It felt the same as when we had sex together, only it lasted several minutes, and it was painful." She looked at Ana to see if her expression changed. "Did I surprise you?" she asked.

"Not at all, Emma. Human experience is wonderful to share." She smiled.

Emma smiled too, and sat back in the chair noticeably more comfortable.

"Marguerite called her mother to our room, and both of them started counting the length of time between what they called contractions."

"Sounds like you were in labor."

"I wasn't quite there yet. In the meantime, Marguerite called my doctor. The contractions lasted all night, and by six in the morning, they were coming about every ten minutes or so. All of a sudden, the bed sheet I was lying on was soaked with liquid. My water had broken. Marguerite told her mother to call the clinic and tell them we were on our way.

"The three of us piled into the Citroën deux chevaux, Marguerite's mother in the back seat and Marguerite and I barely fitting in front. We arrived at the small hospital in the middle of one of my contractions, which forced me to hold tight to Marguerite's arm. I was rushed to the delivery room where the nurse stopped Marguerite from entering.

"'No, no, she comes with me,' I insisted, as I dragged Marguerite through the doors to the astonishment of the nurse who tried to block us. When she saw the look in my eyes, she moved out of the way, and Marguerite was there to stay.

"I was placed on the delivery table, as the nurse started giving orders.

"'Help her breathe,' she told Marguerite, who was holding my hand tightly.

"'Don't push until the doctor tells you to,' the nurse told me.

"'No anesthetic,' I pleaded, even though I was in considerable pain.

"'Deep breaths,' the nurse called out. 'When you have dilated a few more centimeters, we will have to get the doctor in here.'

"And then it was time. The doctor walked in, saw me, grabbed a towel and mopped my brow.

"He said, 'Listen to me: when I say push, you push, and when I say stop, you stop. We don't want you to tear, if we can avoid it. At the appropriate time, I am going to make a small incision that will help with the delivery. I will give you at least a local, if we have time.'

"'Okay for a local,' I stammered, 'but I want to be awake for this blessed event.'

"The doctor made a small incision, and I pushed. And

then, all of a sudden, a baby's head appeared between my legs. I could see the mat of dark hair, covered with slime. The doctor turned the baby's head slightly. I looked over at Marguerite, who was still tense with anticipation, and I pushed again. Then out came a shoulder, then another, and finally the whole body of my little son appeared—perfectly formed.

"The doctor grabbed the baby's feet, and announced, 'It's a boy!' He held him up in the air and whacked his behind. The baby let out a cry, and from then on, he couldn't be quieted until he was put to my breast. While the doctor cut the umbilical cord, I began to lick him and to murmur ancient words that only mothers remember and only another mother would understand.

"I thought of Ian and what he had missed, and I forgave him for not being there, and, at the same time, gave thanks to him for participating in this wonder.

"When the baby took my nipple, I fell into a wave of pleasure, almost beyond sex—and a kind of peace that I had never felt before, but one which I knew I was made to experience. At Marguerite's request, I turned the infant over to her, and she cuddled him in her arms and started sobbing quietly with joy.

"As soon as everything was under control at the hospital, I listened as Marguerite called my father and told him the news. She said that at first he was cold and unresponsive, but when he learned it was a boy and was to be named Alain Janus, his whole attitude changed.

"Before I could catch my breath, I was told that my father had notified all the Polish relatives in the area of Valenciennes. While they were not numerous, they all responded enthusiastically that they wanted to be present at the baptism of my baby boy, which had to take place on the following Sunday."

"That was quite a change for your father, wasn't it?" asked Ana.

"Yes, and I didn't expect it, but as you know better than I, a newborn baby brings inexplicable joy. That is why I cannot imagine my life without him."

"Tell me what happened next," smiled Ana.

"When the day of the baptism arrived, over a hundred people showed up at the Saint-Germain-des-Prés church in Paris. There was a mixture of my Polish and French relatives, a small group representing Marguerite's family, and a number of my friends from school.

"My father, Janus, was the head of the excited and raucous delegation from the north. They were there, bent on celebration, in stark contrast to the Parisians who were more concerned with style and restraint. The Algerian crowd stayed in the background and was discreet about everything. They would smile when smiled upon.

"The priest said his litany in the ancient Latin of the church. In the meantime the bells in the tower tolled because it was a sanctioned baptism performed on a Sunday within eight days of the child's birth. That seemed to be important to my father, although I couldn't figure out why.

"I was told that I looked good in my new dress, even though I couldn't get it all buttoned up. Alain Janus Sheridan was draped in his white baptism attire belonging to the Olech family. My father cuddled him and held him up for the priest. Alain was a little fussy, with the crowd around him, and started crying when the cold water splashed on his forehead. I'm sure he heard the commotion of the bells, and the priest uttering, 'Alain Janus Sheridan, you are becoming a child of God.'"

"That must have been quite a moment, Emma."

"Yes, it was. I was reconnected with my father, who, up until I met Marguerite, was my only ally. The only thing bad that happened that day was that Maurice was in the crowd watching the ceremony."

"Did he approach you?"

"No, he disappeared, and I never saw or heard from him

again except for his attempts to contact me that I've already told you about.

"When the ceremony was complete, my father put an envelope in the priest's hand to express to him the family's gratitude. As I got up from the pew where I had been giving Alain my breast, the bells in the church tower were ringing out the announcement of Alain's baptism. We walked out into the morning sun, and Marguerite's mother was telling everyone that there would be a celebration in their home.

"'Everyone who wants to come, just follow us there. Everyone is welcome,' she announced, and everyone came.

"Back at our flat, my father was the center of attention. He hugged and kissed his week-old grandson and me, and made long speeches in Polish and in French. It was obvious, all was forgiven—he had a grandson. The more shots of vodka he drank, the longer and more colorful the speeches became. I sat quietly in a corner, talking with Marguerite about how to care for the baby and smiling and sharing my pride with her relatives while the Algerian women huddled in the kitchen, preparing all kinds of Arabic food and a few Polish dishes as well.

"There was music. My father, who loved to dance, first invited Marguerite to join him, and then he twirled as many women around as he could entice onto the makeshift dance floor.

"Marguerite had a few moments with me during that afternoon. I told her I couldn't thank her enough for what she had done for me and my son, and I kissed her on the lips to let the world know that I loved her, even though we'd been living openly together for most of my pregnancy.

"She said, 'our son,' as she took Alain in her arms and twirled him around our bedroom."

"What a wonderful memory, Emma."

"Thank you." Smiling broadly and taking a deep breath

Emma said, "You see his birth has been the most important event in my life. It's also important because it brought my father back to me. Losing Alain would have been beyond what I could handle."

"He's home now. Are you having difficulty with him because of the kidnapping?"

"He is quite buttoned up anyway, as you know. He won't confide in me at all, so I don't know how the kidnapping has affected him. Pile that on top of losing his father after he came back into his life, and I worry about him."

"That's why I want to start counseling him."

"The losses in his life are not his only problem."

"Yes, I'm aware of that," said Ana. "I have had experience with children like him. But I can tell from talking with him today that he is a very special boy. I will treat him with care, don't worry."

14

The Victims

Samuel thought carefully about how to approach the difficult task of getting statements from the boys at Towne School. He needed to get information without frightening them or leaving them with the impression that they could be the next victims. His decided to go directly to the homes of the boys who had been close friends of the decedents so the entire school would not know who had been questioned.

Before he went, he studied the file. First, he looked at the school photos of the two murdered boys. They were both eleven years old, the same age as Alain, and in the sixth grade. Bruce Axelrod had dark hair and a glint in his eyes that suggested he was devilish. Phillip Atkinson appeared more circumspect. He had the look of a future Montgomery Street executive with his brown hair neatly parted in the middle, a cautious smile, and perfect teeth. Their school files showed they were both excellent students in all subjects. Bruce had exceptional skills in mathematics and science. He also had an IQ that was ten points higher than his companion Phillip. But marring their otherwise spotless records, Samuel noted that both had received disciplinary warnings a couple of months before their deaths.

His first visit was to the home of John McPherson who

he was told was the best friend of Phillip Atkinson. He lived with his family in Pacific Heights on Broadway near Divisadero. It was a spectacular neighborhood, each house a standout. This one was no exception—a perfectly trimmed brown shingle home with a view of the bay, which, on the day of Samuel's visit, was sparkling with sailboats and ships moving in and out through the Golden Gate. The view was for the privileged. His appointment was for four o'clock, just after the boy came home from school. He was ushered into the parlor by the boy's mother, who cut a smart figure in a stylish blouse and skirt that appeared to be perfectly tailored from The City of Paris or I. Magnin. Samuel had called the mother ahead of time, so she'd prepared the boy for the interview. John came downstairs, already changed from his school uniform, dressed in jeans and a T-shirt.

He was of medium height and had reddish blond hair, a face full of freckles, and a gap between his front teeth. Samuel shook his limp hand and the boy sat down next to his mother who was noticeably nervous.

"Thanks for seeing me this afternoon, John." Samuel sought to put the boy at ease. "I need to ask you some questions about your friend Phillip. I understand the two of you were best of friends."

"Yeah, me and Phil did a lot of things together."

"How are you getting along with all that's happened?"

"Pretty much like the rest of the kids at school. Some good days and some bad ones. I felt very nervous when the killer was still out there. But after we heard that they caught him, we stopped being so scared."

"Who did you hear that from?"

"From Tony Patruski. He said his dad had captured the guy who did it, and we shouldn't worry anymore. That was a big relief." He sighed loudly and slumped in his seat.

"Is Tony a friend of yours?"

"I know him because we go to school together. He and Phillip were best friends. Closer than I was. They used to hang around after school and had overnights together."

"Did you ever join them?"

"No. Like I said, they were the ones that were close."

"What was your relationship with Bruce Axelrod, the other boy who was killed?"

"We used to be good friends. I was closer to him than I was to Phillip."

"What can you tell me about him?" Samuel asked. "You say you used to be friends. What changed?"

The boy thought for a few seconds and squinted. "I don't know," he stalled. "He changed."

"Changed, how?"

"It's, like, something changed in him."

"Can you explain that to me?"

"He became distant—at least from me. It seemed like something was bothering him."

"Did he ever confide in you about what was going on?"

"No. Like I said, we weren't spending that much time together anymore. He, Phillip, and Tony were hanging around with each other all of the time, and I was busy with school."

"It sounds like they pushed you out of their circle."

He shrugged, looking down at the expensive Persian carpet.

His mother blurted out, "You know how cliquish young people can be," and she put her arm around her son.

Samuel smiled at her and nodded his agreement. "Just a few more questions, John. What's your relationship like with Tony since Bruce's death?"

He shrugged again. "It's okay, I guess. But you know two of our classmates were killed. It's hard to get over something like that."

His mother squirmed in her seat. She obviously wanted

the interview to end.

"I'm almost finished, Mrs. McPherson," Samuel promised. He offered an apologetic smile before he returned to his questioning. "Has Tony said anything to you about the death of either of your friends?"

"Not much. He seemed totally shocked just like the rest of us. Since then, we've all drifted further apart. It's sort of like everyone has gone into his own shell."

"Is there anything you can think of that might be a clue to who killed your friends other than what you heard from Tony that the killer was in jail?"

"I've told you everything I know," said John with a sad look on his freckled face.

Samuel knew that the interview was over, so he thanked John and his mother, and he left. He walked down the block and sank onto a bus stop bench deep in thought, trying to put together what he had learned about the split up between the friends and wondering where Tony fit into the puzzle. Sitting there waiting for the bus gave him time to let the heaviness of the interview filter out of him before he went to the other boy's home.

Steven Jones had also been a friend of the murdered boys. Just like John, he reported having noticed a change in the behavior of Bruce Axelrod a few weeks before his death. He confirmed that there were no other boys in the school who had been as connected as Tony Patruski to the two victims. He also said that Bruce told him that he wasn't going to hang around with Tony anymore.

"Did he say why?" Samuel pressed.

"No, he only mentioned it in passing, but he looked pretty upset."

"When was this?"

"A couple of weeks before he was killed."

Samuel wanted to continue the questioning, but the boy

was visually upset. "I'm sorry, Mr. Hamilton, that's it. That's all I have to offer."

Samuel wondered if the boy was hiding something, but he couldn't go on, so he left.

Samuel's next stop was at the flat of a teacher, Miss Madeline Jansen. All four boys plus Tony had been in her class the first two hours of the morning for civics and history.

A tall, slender woman with dark hair hanging to her shoulders, she had blue eyes, a fair complexion, and a ready smile, but behind those pleasant features was an intensely suspicious aura. She lived in the Richmond District on Twenty-Eighth Avenue near Clement in a stucco row house with the typical iron gate and buzzer that kept unwanted company from entering. Her house was a big comedown from the ones her students lived in.

Nevertheless, when she invited Samuel in for a cup of coffee, he saw that it was comfortable and in good taste. They sat in two armchairs, looking out the bay window and watching the fog rolling in from the ocean moving towards the east.

Samuel took out his notebook and leaned back in one of the overstuffed chairs. He explained that he had just talked to John and Steven about what they recalled of the two murdered boys. He noticed that she was sitting on the edge of the other chair.

"In particular, John mentioned how Phillip had been closest to Bruce, and he also commented that he, John, felt excluded from the relationship that Bruce, Tony, and Phillip had developed before Bruce's death. It seems that the two murdered boys and Tony spent more time together than with the other boys in the class until a couple of weeks before Bruce's death, when Bruce decided he didn't want anything more to do with Tony. That's what John said Bruce told him, in any case."

Miss Jansen finally relaxed into her chair. "I'm really glad you talked to those boys, Mr. Hamilton. I'm going to be frank with you. I've been waiting for someone to contact me. The deaths were a big blow to the school. It certainly doesn't want any bad publicity. So, I want our conversation to be private for now, and I need for you to respect that before we go on."

"Of course," said Samuel. "I will respect your confidentiality. Please go ahead."

"I was worried about both boys for a couple of months before their deaths. Both were acting out in class. That was something neither had done before. I was about to call their parents and have a talk with them to see if we could get to the bottom of it. In the meantime, I talked to Mr. Gravestone. He had the boys later in the day for biology."

"Tell me about Mr. Gravestone."

"I asked him if he'd noticed any change in either of the boys."

"What did he say?"

"That he had noticed the hostility with which they both treated fellow students. He also said that they began acting out in class. He'd even sent them to the principal's office a couple of times, but he didn't think they were out of control or anything like that. 'Just kids,' he said.

"After their deaths, I told the principal about their behavior, and he said he would pass it on to the police, but I don't know if he did or not," she said in an agitated tone. "Anyway, I'm glad to share it with you."

"I'm a reporter, Miss Jansen, and I live off my tips. I always protect my sources, I promise you. Can you give me some examples of how they acted out?"

"First of all, Bruce started brooding and scowling a lot. He was brilliant in mathematics and science, and he'd always been a fairly happy kid before then. Phillip Atkinson was also smart—maybe not quite as smart as Bruce, but they hung around together. Their friendship made sense. Within a few months of the time they were killed, they started palling around with Tony Patruski, the policeman's son. He was just a fun guy that everybody liked. But you know, he was older than the other boys by a couple of years, and he wasn't a good student. He had a chip on his shoulder because of his father's position, and he probably led them into things that they weren't ready to experience."

"Can you be more specific than that?"

"Not really, because I didn't see them together off the school grounds, but I wanted to alert you to his influence on them.

"Both boys started slacking off, not turning in class work, severing connections with the other boys. Bruce, much more than Phillip. When they did interact with the other students, they were overly aggressive, picking fights and bullying the younger boys in the school who unintentionally got in their paths. I had to send them to the principal's office on more than one occasion."

"What do you think was going on?"

"Just between you and me, I always thought that Bruce may have had a sexual identity problem, and I wondered if he was after Phillip as a potential sexual partner. That's the part I don't want you to say you got from me. But I don't have any proof of that. It's just speculation. Just as I don't want you to mention that I thought Tony was a troublemaker, because I don't have any hard facts to prove it."

"I understand," said Samuel. "Tell me about their behavior in class."

"It was the same as I described with the younger boys. They would push and shove smaller boys for no apparent reason and even hit them. I had to break up a fist fight that Bruce had with another student, and Phillip piled on him too. It was something the other student said, and none of them would tell me what it was."

"Who was the student that called Bruce the name?" asked

Samuel.

"I believe it was Charles Hancock."

"How much of that can be chalked up to their age—you know, boys will be boys, that kind of thing? Like Mr. Gravestone said."

"This was way beyond that, and it was such a change from how they'd been before. There was something wrong."

"Did the principal say anything about hearing the same thing from other teachers like Mr. Gravestone?"

"No, apparently I was the only teacher to come to him complaining about their behavior."

"Does the school have a psychologist?"

"They have one on call, Doctor Friedman."

"Did you mention their behavior to him?"

"Yes, I did. He was going to have a session with each one of them. But we had to first get their parents' permission, and they were killed before that could be arranged."

"Did you talk with him after their deaths?"

"Yes, I did. He took notes and said he would inquire further and write a report. But if he did, I have no knowledge of it."

"You look frustrated," said Samuel.

"We're a small and elite school. This was a terrible blow to us. All the boys in the school were victims of the result of these crimes. And, so far, there is no resolution. It's such an awful shame what happened to those two boys. I hope you can help catch whoever did this."

"I take it, you're in the camp that thinks that the killer has not been captured?"

"If he has, it certainly hasn't been in the press."

Samuel nodded. "I wouldn't be here if the killer had been captured. Thanks for talking to me. You can be sure I will keep your observations in confidence. But I do want Lieutenant Bernardi to know about the behavior. I think he can get that from the psychologist's report, if one exists. But if not, I'll have to bring him back to talk with you. Can you think of anyone else that I could talk with that could give me an insight to the boys or their behavior?"

"The only other person I can think of was both boys' math tutor. As I said they were both extraordinary talents in math, and they used the same tutor."

"Is it a he or a she?"

"It's a man."

"Can you give me his name and address or a phone number?"

"Yes, I have it here. His name is Mitchell Harbano, and his phone number is SU 4-3268."

"Thank you," said Samuel.

She nodded her head reluctantly as she extended her hand. "I hope I've been some help to you."

* * *

When Samuel left the teacher's apartment he took the bus downtown, switched to a Hyde Street cable car, and went up the hill for a nightcap at Camelot. He sat down at the Round Table and gave Excalibur a treat while Melba listened carefully to what he recounted.

"Sounds like you had a rough day, cowboy. Let me turn this over in my head." Melba took a drag on her Lucky Strike. "Next time I see you, I'll tell you what I think," she said reassuringly.

Samuel finished his second drink, then went down the street to his apartment on the edge of Chinatown where he fell into bed, exhausted.

The next morning he went directly to Bernardi's office at the Hall of Justice. Bernardi showed up fifteen minutes later, and they huddled in Bernardi's office going over what Samuel had learned from the two boys and the teacher. They looked at the file together, trying to put everything in place. In the mean time, a secretary brought coffee in paper cups for both men.

"The most important lead I got was from the teacher. She started talking about Bruce Axelrod's sexual identity problems. No one else ever mentioned that. She also told me that she thought Tony was two years older than his friends and a troublemaker. In other words he's already a teenager, and, no doubt, dealing with raging hormones."

"I see there is a report from the psychologist, but it's very brief," said Bernardi. "It doesn't mention sexual identity, or acting out either."

"The sexuality thing is a touchy subject. I think that you're going to have to follow up on it with the psychologist and the teachers," said Samuel. "I'm sure none of them will talk to me about the boys' emotional state, or their sexual identities. But they can't ignore you, since you represent police business."

Bernardi pursed his lips, nodded, then took a sip of his morning coffee.

"In addition, you should be the one to approach Tony Patruski because his father won't let me near him," said Samuel. "Especially since he's let everybody know that he's already caught the killer."

"Let's think about this for a minute," said Bernardi. "That may be why Patruski is so anxious to charge Levantine with the murders. Maybe he knows Tony was involved sexually with Bruce Axelrod, and he doesn't want anyone to find out about that."

Samuel turned his notebook back to the teacher's statement about it, showing Bernardi.

"You have a point. It's been bothering me that Patruski is pushing such a weak case against Levantine. What I've learned from the two friends and especially the teacher makes it pretty obvious we're not getting the whole story."

Samuel stood up. "I think we should see if we can find out more about the sexual identity problem, and I'd rather you waited until we have a better idea on that before you talk to Tony. Also, you need to talk with the parents of the murdered boys. Let's see if they can fill us in on this issue. It will make a big difference about where we go in this investigation."

"Yeah, you're right," said Bernardi. "Something is still out there waiting for us. But we have to get to Tony before Patruski tries to convince the DA to charge Levantine with the murders. If that happens, he won't let us get near Tony."

"Can he do that? You're in charge of homicide, not him."

"You know about back door politics. That happens even in police departments."

"This guy could create a mess, couldn't he?" said Samuel. "I think you need to have a talk with the DA and point out the difference between Alain and the two victims. Tell him Levantine's side of the story. Explain that he believed the boy was his son. That should hold him off."

"Patruski says he wants to close the book on all three kidnappings, and he can't do that if the murders are classified as unsolved crimes."

"This is beginning to bother me a lot," said Samuel. His face was drawn, and he was rubbing his hands. "If Patruski tries to stop you from getting to his son's involvement with the other boys, and he gets you sacked, I'm in deep shit."

Bernardi laughed and winked at Samuel. "Don't worry. I trust the DA. It's not going to get that far. I have a stronger relationship with him than Patruski does."

"Okay, I hope you're right. Can I go with you when you talk to the psychologist and the other teachers?" asked Samuel.

"Sure, let me set up the appointments."

"There is one other lead I need to follow up on, the math tutor. If he gives me any trouble or won't talk to me, I'll need your help. In the meantime, I'll check back with Mac and see what the forensic tests tell us," said Samuel.

"Looks like we have our work cut out for us," said Bernardi.

"There's one thing I want to check out before I forget," said Samuel.

"What's that?"

Samuel stood up, almost ready to leave. "The supermarket where each of the murdered boys went to get a snack on the days they disappeared. The statements from the employees are pretty perfunctory. I'll go over there and ask some more questions, but I may need your help, if management gets in the way."

"Anything you need from me is yours," said Bernardi.

* * *

Alain and Emma walked through Ana's garden into the consultation room. Emma left him there and retired to the garden with a book

Ana did not try and give Alain a hug because she knew how he felt about being touched. She pointed him to the rocking chair, and he sat down stiffly.

"I studied your goddess and Walt Whitman too," Alain said. "Did you know that Whitman is considered by many as America's most important poet?"

"That doesn't surprise me. I just found those words so inviting and so important that I had to copy them onto my garden wall."

"Did you ever read *Leaves of Grass*?" he asked.

"I must admit that I haven't read it in its entirety, but when we have more time, you can tell me about it. I want to go over some things with you today that I feel are important. Is that all right with you?" asked Ana as she leaned towards him from her rocking chair.

"That's why I came," he said, giving her as much of a smile as he was capable of. "My mother told me you could help me get over what has happened in the past few weeks. I'm not sure I need help, but I'm willing to listen to what you have to say."

"I'm not here to tell you anything, Alain. We're just going to have a conversation and see where it leads. Is that all right with you?"

"Okay."

"Can you tell me something of your early life with your mother? I know your father wasn't there when you were small."

"My father wasn't there with us then, but my grandfather was, and I was very close to him. He taught me how to read, and he would build things with me. I love him very much, and I miss him now, because he is so far away."

"He comes to visit you, doesn't he?"

"Oh, yes. In fact, he is coming next week. I am very happy about that."

"When did you first meet your father?"

"I was about six. My mother and I came to California to meet him, and we stayed. That wasn't part of the original plan, but it worked out that way. My grandmother Reyna Henri came to live with us after my aunt Marguerite, my second mother, died. I was happy to learn about my father and to be with him. He and I and my grandfather had the same interests. Unfortunately, it was only for a short time. A couple of years ago, my father went to Vietnam, and he never came back. He was killed in action. They sent us an American flag and a war medal."

"How did you feel about all that?"

"I was just starting to get to know him, and he left. The man I am closest to is my grandfather. I spent a lot of time with him when I was young. He taught me how to build boxes and fit them together with the right joints. He taught me about the universe and bragged that Copernicus, who was also Polish like us, was the first one to explain that the sun was at the center of the universe instead of the earth, but he had to keep it secret, because he was a priest and the Catholic Church teachings at that time was that the earth was the center of the universe. You know what happened to Galileo for making the same claim.

"I used to sit in my grandfather's lap, and he would teach me algebra. I missed him when we left France for America. My mother told me that Ian was my father, and that's why we came here, to be with him. He treated me very nicely, and when he learned what my grandfather had taught me, he expanded on it and explained more of the universe to me. For instance, he told me that Kepler showed the world about how the orbits of the planets were elliptical. This helped further prove that the earth orbited around the sun.

"When Maurice took me and told me he was my father, I got angry. I knew he was lying because he wouldn't have treated me so badly if he really thought that I was his son. Both my grandfather and Ian were super compared to him."

"I want to talk to you about being kidnapped. Your experience reminded me of the story of Hansel and Gretel. Do you know it?" asked Ana.

"I remember it from my childhood."

"Tell me what you remember."

"The boy, Hansel, and his sister, Gretel, were tricked into leaving home by a cruel mother who convinced their passive father to help her because they couldn't even feed themselves, let alone the children. The parents took them deep into the forest and helped them build a fire and left some food for them, never intending to see them again. But Hansel, who was very clever, put down shiny pebbles on the way. When the moon came out, it shone brightly upon the pebbles, which illuminated their way back home.

"When times got bad again, the mother convinced the father to take Hansel and Gretel deeper into the forest. This time, Hansel laid down crumbs as a way of finding their way back. However, after spending a cold night in the forest, they couldn't find their way back home the next day because birds had eaten the crumbs."

"You remember this story from childhood?"

"Oh yes, my grandfather is a wonderful story-teller. He told it to me and it's still vivid in my mind."

"I'm sorry, go on."

"Hansel and Gretel wandered in the woods for a few days until they came across a gingerbread house, and they started eating it, little by little, until the owner came out and invited them in for a real meal. It turned out that she was a wicked witch and very soon enslaved them. She locked Hansel up and intended to cook him as soon as he was fattened up, and she had Gretel feed him through a slot in his cell door. Hansel fooled her and kept sticking a bone out the crack when she asked to feel his finger. You see, she was a witch who had very poor eyesight.

"When she got tired of waiting, she had Gretel prepare a cauldron with boiling water over the fire so she could cook Hansel. Gretel tricked her into looking into the cauldron while the water was boiling, and since it was tilted at the perfect geometrical angle, Gretel kicked her into it, thus saving Hansel's life."

"My goodness, then what happened?"

"The children looked through the house and found jewels and riches and carried away as much as they could. They made their way back to their parents' home where they found out that their mother had died, so they lived happily ever after with their father."

"What did you think of the story?"

"It was a fairy tale. I was happy that the kids survived. I thought both their parents were pretty bad, if that's what you're looking for." Alain stood up and asked for a drink of water. Ana poured one for him from a pitcher she had at her side, and he drank it down in one gulp.

"Does the story have a deeper meaning for you?"

"I'm not sure what you're asking," he frowned.

"Do you see any parallel to your being kidnapped?"

"Oh, I see what you mean. I never thought about it until right now. Well yes, I had studied many things when I was very young, and all of those things helped me escape from my kidnapper and survive until I was rescued."

"Can you give me some examples?"

"I studied the Sea Scouts knot tying book. I studied *The Boy Scout Handbook* and the army survival manuals. And my favorite book is *Robinson Crusoe.* They all helped me a lot. First I tied the knots to slide down from the window. Then I used army tactics to build myself shelter and to erase my path, so I couldn't be followed by my kidnapper. And, I used what I learned from the survival field manual to find food and to cook what I found in nature. I also took a bear rug to keep me warm."

"I think you actually lived the story of Hansel and Gretel."

"What do you mean?"

"You learned how to take care of yourself when you needed to."

"Oh, I see. It's kind of nice that I could, isn't it?"

"You sound as if you understood the pebbles that glowed in the moonlight were very important, and that you have them in your memory for when you need to use them."

"You think so?"

"Have you ever thought why you learned all the things you talk about?"

"Not specifically. I have just been interested in them from the time I was very young."

"Do you think your mother has anything to do with your journey?"

"I'm not sure what you mean."

"Isn't she the most important person in your life?"

"By far," he said, with a quizzical look on his face. "Are you saying that I learned all those things in order to protect her?"

"I'm not saying anything, I'm just asking questions. Why don't you think about all those things? We'll go over them again when we meet next time. And, we'll talk about your father, if you want to," and she took his hand and squeezed it. "But before you go, let me say once again that your journey, like Hansel and Gretel's, was very remarkable."

"I never thought about it before. But I see what you're driving at. I was prepared," and he laughed a short unusual laugh. One that, Ana could tell, he wasn't accustomed to.

"By the way, your mother told me you had a very keen sense about animals. Can you tell me if that helped you when you were in mountains?"

"Yes, it did help me. You see, I feel very comfortable around animals. So when I saw bears, mountain lions, and foxes in the wild, I wasn't afraid. We just sort of shared the space and left each other alone."

Ana smiled, took his hand again, and led him to the door. She called Emma in from the garden. "Thank you for sharing Alain with me. He is a very special person, and we got a lot done today."

15

The Sordid Reality

SAMUEL WOKE UP IN THE middle of the night and sat at the edge of his fold-up bed. He looked out the dirty kitchen window at the street below, littered with yesterday's papers and other items of trash from the markets of Chinatown and the impolite discards of the population in general. Sweat dripped from his brow. His thoughts spun while he tried to digest all the information he'd gathered in the last few days. He couldn't connect any of it in a meaningful way. It was as if he had his hands in a bowl of mush. He needed a new approach to evaluate the evidence of the two murders and settled on the person he could ask for help—the psychiatrist who'd treated him when he was in a deep depression after his parents were murdered several years back. But first, he needed some more information. He would seek out Phillip McIntosh and go over the evidence with him again. Then he would have the meeting with the doctor.

Before starting his day he stopped for an early morning cappuccino and croissant at the Café Trieste, where he caught up on several Herb Caen columns he hadn't had a chance to read. Then he took the bus to the Hall of Justice and waited in the forensic lab to talk with Mac.

When Mac arrived, Samuel said hello and asked if he

could go over the results on the human excrement that they had found in the alleyway.

Mac went to the evidence locker and brought back the containers and his report. "You're fast, Samuel. I was going to turn the reports over to Bernardi today."

"Give me the good news," said Samuel, laughing. "If there is any."

"Don't know what to make of these two piles other than they're from the same person. Whoever it is eats a lot of hot dogs or sausage."

"Can you tell if it's a male or a female?"

"Assuming that a female wouldn't eat hot dogs or sausages, I'd say it was a man."

"What kind of sausage?"

"I looked it up, and the closest I came to pinning it down was that it has the same ingredients as Polish sausage."

Samuel's head snapped back. "You're kidding?" Patruski was from a Polish background.

"No, it's either that or hot dogs. I'll have to do more tests and ask some questions, but that's the way it looks."

"What about the tire track?"

"It's not from the standard fleet of police cars. They use only Goodyear tires, and this tread mark is not from one them, or even from a Goodyear tire. I stopped looking when I found that out because there are so many cars and so many makes of tires that I'd be doing nothing else for a month. If you come back to me with a specific car model, I can help you—otherwise, it's just a random motorist backing out or visiting the alley on some kind of business."

Samuel didn't like the response but walked out of the lab in a hurry, shaking his head. He felt that the fact that only one tire had passed through the fecal matter was important, but he decided he would deal with it later. He went up to Bernardi's office to tell him what he'd found out, but Bernardi wasn't there, so he left a note. Then he hurried to Third and Townsend to catch the train for the appointment with his former psychiatrist. He looked out the window as the train sped southward. His mind was spinning about what Mac had told him, even though Mac wasn't sure about the meat scraps being Polish sausage. He started going over Patruski's actions since the kidnapping of Alain and putting the pieces together. They could point to Patruski as the perpetrator.

He got off at the Burlingame station and arrived on time for his appointment. He took a seat and gave his name to the receptionist, then waited for her to invite him in to see the doctor. Marvin Vishinski was sitting at a desk writing some notes on his visit with his last patient, but he immediately stood up to greet Samuel and shake his hand. He hadn't changed much. He had a thick mane of gray hair, a full beard, and a large black mole on his left cheek. He wore horn-rimmed glasses. He always reminded Samuel of Captain Nemo, right out of a Jules Verne novel.

"It's wonderful to see you, Samuel. I hope you're doing well. I assume you're doing well because you haven't been back to see me until now. I read about your ventures in the newspaper, and aside from getting fired a year or so ago, it's all positive. I saw that you started a new job with the afternoon paper, so I bet you made whatever happened work to your advantage. I often talk about you, without mentioning your name, of course. I use you as an example for many of my patients, especially those who are clinically depressed. I tell them how you faced adversity and how you apparently overcame it and made a new life for yourself."

Samuel kept silent until he got an opening. "Thanks, Doc. I couldn't have done it without you. But I really didn't come here to talk about myself. I'll leave that for another day. I have a serious problem in a case that I'm working on, and I thought you could help me by giving me some advice on what to look for."

The doctor sat down at his desk and took out a note pad. "Okay, tell me what you want me to consider?"

Samuel sat down on the other side of the desk and also took out his notebook. He gave the doctor the history of the two murdered boys, explaining how they were killed after they were molested sexually, and talked about the rambling ransom notes that were presented with really no intention of trying to collect a ransom. Then, he explained finding two piles of dried excrement in the alleyway, left by the same person. "So my first question is, assuming these piles were left by the person who killed both boys, what does that mean?"

The doctor took off his glasses and placed them on the desk beside his notepad. "My goodness, you are looking for a very sick person. It's probably a man, and he has had a very difficult childhood. You need to look for a history of cruelty to animals, abnormal behavior in school, and a really miserable connection to society. The defecation in the alleyway is very common of this kind of psychotic. He marks his territory. In addition, as a child, he was probably a fire starter."

"Could this person be a policeman?"

"He would have to have changed his name and hidden his past in order not to have it show up. I'm sure the authorities would check up on that. So, it's possible, but very unlikely. Furthermore, if he is on the police force, your first job would be to get him off of it immediately because he's bound to commit more crimes like this."

"I take it that the sexual part is very important?"

"Oh yes, this man is a predator, he combines sex and injury together. In fact, it's a classic case with those two characteristics."

Samuel thanked the doctor, left, and went directly to the train station. He got back to San Francisco around noon.

* * *

Bernardi was waiting in his office when Samuel arrived. Samuel told him all that had transpired, including his meeting with Mac and his discussion with the doctor about what they were looking for.

"It's pretty easy to check up on Patruski. He's been on the force for almost fifteen years, and he has a spotless record," said Bernardi. "I checked on that when I read your note from this morning."

"Could he have doctored his record?"

"Well, that's possible. He's from the Chicago area. There is a large Polish population there. But they look into these things very carefully and from what you described that one should expect from such a person, we have no information that he has a history of being a sexual deviant, a fire starter, or an animal killer."

"So you think that it's more likely he's trying to protect his son than anything else?"

Bernardi nodded. "Protecting his son's reputation. It's terrible to expose someone as a homosexual, even in San Francisco. There are consequences that follow a person for the rest of his life."

Samuel pounded his fist into his open hand. "I think Patruski is hiding something else. It's just a hunch at this point, but I can't let it go. Maybe you should go to Chicago and check out his background while I check out the employees and the math tutor."

"Not yet. I want to show the DA that we're doing something and that it will take time to get results."

They looked at each other, neither wanting to give ground. Then Samuel spoke. "I don't think we can hold off much longer on getting something on Patruski because he's closing in on Levantine, and this case might blow up in our face if the DA decides to prosecute Levantine instead of the real murderer."

"We can't just accuse Patruski of trying to frame Levantine.

We have to show the DA that the evidence doesn't point to him, and there's a greater probability that someone else did it," said Bernardi. "A forensic report that someone's crap had fragments of Polish sausage isn't enough."

"Don't you think it's important that both murdered boys were sexually assaulted, and Alain wasn't?"

"Yeah. That's what's stopping me from siding with Patruski. But, so far, you haven't made that crystal clear to me. Did you ask him that?"

"I didn't go into that because I was sure he wasn't."

"Since I'm the boss, here's what I want you do," Bernardi said with a stern look on his face and pointing a finger at Samuel. "You take statements from the math tutor and the employees at the market, and I'll take the parents, the remaining teachers, and the psychologist, and let's see what we come up with. In addition, you ask Alain and his mother if he was sexually molested by the Frenchman. Then we'll sit down with the DA and maybe even Patruski."

Samuel realized he'd lost the battle and that he had made a big mistake in not asking Alain what was turning out to be a key question. "Will you at least check further on Patruski's background, or let me go to Chicago and do it, just to make sure we're not overlooking anything or anyone, and can you find out what kind of car Patruski drives?"

"I'll get those things done. Write down what the doctor told you we should look for. If I don't have time to go to Chicago, I'll send you to look into Patruski's past."

Samuel walked out of Bernardi's office and went down to the coffee shop in the basement. He stirred the weak coffee with a spoon while he stared at the wall. He felt worse than before he spoke to Bernardi. He realized that implicating a cop wouldn't go over well, and he expected some kind of resistance, but not this much. He wondered if he could go to Chicago on his own to investigate Patruski's past. But if he could show that the tire mark matched the brand of tires on Patruski's personal vehicle it would make a difference. He knew he couldn't get far without Bernardi's help, so he stopped staring at the wall, took a sip of his watered-down coffee, and wrote down who he was going to interview and when.

He decided he would go first to the market on California Street where both boys said they were going for snacks before they went missing. He also called Mitchell Harbano, the math tutor, at the phone number that the teacher had given him, but the phone had been disconnected. He decided he would worry about that later since he already had his hands full. Then he called Emma and told her to get Alain back to Ana Cejas for more questions about whether he was sexually molested by Levantine. "Did he say anything to you about that?" asked Samuel. "He never mentioned it to the police."

"He didn't say anything to me about that. He would have told me if he had."

"We have to ask him, Emma. It's a very important question now. I'll explain later."

"You can't ask me to probe my child with a question like that without giving me a good reason, Samuel."

"You're right. I'm sorry." He took a deep breath. "Both the murdered boys were sexually assaulted. Patruski is trying to accuse Levantine of their murder, and if he can show that Alain was sexually attacked also, he wins the battle to put Levantine on trial. I'm trying to save the man's life. I want you to help me by asking Alain."

"I understand now," said Emma. "I will ask him and explain to Ana what you are trying to find out. Thank you for being honest with me Samuel. Even though I am very angry with Maurice, I also don't think that he is that kind of a man."

Samuel caught the Sacramento bus west until Pacific Heights. He got off and went directly to the market on California Street and asked to see the manager. They sat together in a cramped office at the rear of the market next to a large parking lot. The man was in his fifties, bald, and had a harried look on his face. The market was packed with shoppers, some of whom continually walked by the open door as the two talked. Samuel explained that he was a reporter and that two teenage boys had disappeared after they told their parents they were coming to the market to buy afternoon snacks. He gave the manager the dates of their disappearance, and pulled out the manager's statement that he had given to the police soon after their deaths. The manager looked over his desk at the typed paper in Samuel's hand.

"As I told the police, I have no recollection of seeing either boy at any time in this store."

"That's what your statement says, but let me show you their photos. Does that refresh your recollection that maybe you did?"

The bald-headed man shook his head. "Doesn't help me. I don't recognize either of them. "Do you want to talk to the cashiers who were on duty on those dates at the time you indicate?"

"If you don't mind."

"Well, I do mind, but we want to help out if we can. You understand, this is a business, and we're usually swamped because this is where Pacific Heights shops."

"I understand, and if you can just give me a few minutes of their time, I'll get out of here."

The manager funneled the cashiers into his office one by one. Three of them recognized the boys, but none had seen them on the days they disappeared. And none had ever seen the boys leave with anyone else. Then Samuel asked to interview the box boys. All of them except one were there, but none of them had seen anything either.

Samuel thanked the manager and left the market. He went directly to a phone booth and called the teacher, Miss Jansen, explaining that the tutor's phone had been disconnected. "I did hear that he left the state and went home to Georgia, I believe that's where he was from."

"Do you know when that was?"

"No, I just heard that in passing from one of the boys. In fact it was Charles Hancock, the one I told you about that had called Phillip a queer."

"By the way, do you know if he owned a car?"

"I assume so, but I never saw it. Ask one of the boys that he tutored."

"Like Charles Hancock?"

"I think he was one of his pupils."

"Thank you, Miss Jansen. I'll be back in touch."

* * *

It was now late in the afternoon. Samuel was tired and disappointed about the way the day had gone, so he went to Camelot to see if he could talk things over with Melba. When he arrived she was sitting at the Round Table drinking a beer with Excalibur at her side. The dog jumped with excitement when he saw Samuel, and the reporter didn't disappoint him, throwing him a treat and scratching his head.

"You look like shit, Samuel. Sit down and have a drink."

"Thanks, I need one."

Samuel spent a good half hour explaining to her what had transpired since he'd last seen her and how unexpectedly sex had become the most important issue in the case. "Are you telling me this because all of a sudden you and Bernardi realized that there's a whole lot of it going on?"

Samuel let out a half-hearted laugh. "No, I'm telling you that the issue is now important because if Levantine didn't molest Alain, I can help save his life. Otherwise he's fucked. He's going to be gassed."

"I get you," said Melba, turning serious. "What does Alain's mother say?"

"She said that Alain didn't say anything about being molested, and that if he had been, he would have told her."

"What's wrong with that as an answer?"

"Maybe he was ashamed to tell her."

"You're really not looking for sex, Samuel. The other boys were killed. Even if this Maurice fellow molested him, he didn't kill him."

"Patruski will argue that the boy escaped too soon."

"Did Patruski say anything about Alain being molested in his report?"

"No."

"That means to me that he asked him, and the boy said no."

"That's what I think too," said Samuel, "but now I have a feeling that he will claim that the boy is ashamed, and that is why he's not admitting it. He wants Levantine tried for those murders."

"You and Bernardi can handle that son of a bitch. Threaten to take a statement from his son. That will shut him up." She laughed smugly, took a swig of her beer, and lit a Lucky Strike. "I had another thought, it's about the market. If neither the cashiers nor the box boys recognized either of those boys, and the parents claimed they went there for snacks, it means to me they didn't go there. That's the fib they told their parents to meet the killer, who they obviously already knew and trusted."

Samuel put his scotch down on the oak table, took a deep breath, and looked intensely at Melba. "That's a great observation, Melba. I was so stuck on the story, and so anxious to find whoever did this, that I couldn't stray from the police report," he said as he smiled and opened his eyes wide in acknowledgement. "Of course that's the answer, they never went to the store. That's what they each said to get out of the house."

16

A Delicate Inquiry

Emma rushed to her appointment with Ana. "I'm sorry to have called you on such short notice," said Ana, "but there have been some developments in Alain's case that require me to ask him some sensitive questions, and I wanted to alert you first." She went on to explain that there was a question of whether Alain was sexually molested by Maurice.

"I am sure he was not," said Emma. "That is the first thing he would have told me."

"Did you ask him that directly?"

"No. Of course I didn't. It wasn't necessary."

"You understand that I have to explore this with him."

"Yes, Samuel explained it all to me."

"Okay, we know that Maurice's life depends on it, because the two other boys that were kidnapped were sexually molested before they were killed, and if Maurice molested Alain, the authorities will try him for their deaths," said Ana.

"Do you really understand my son? He can't stand to be touched by other people. If Maurice had tried to touch him in any sexual way, he would have become hysterical, and then the only way for Maurice to quiet him would have been to kill him. When he came back home he had scrapes and scratches from his escape but nothing from a human hand."

"I'll be very careful with him, Emma, but I must ask the question."

Emma was quiet for a moment. "Can I be present when you ask him?"

Ana shook her head. "I'd prefer that you weren't. Parents can affect the outcome of questions like that, and I need to be able to testify to his answers, if that becomes necessary."

Emma relented. "Okay. When do you want to see him?"

"It's Saturday. How about this afternoon at three o'clock?"

"Can we make it at two? Once you have talked to him, I would like to come back and talk with you myself."

"Very well. I'll see him at two, and then talk to you after I finish with him."

"I'll need a few minutes to walk him home and come back."

"Just have him bring a book, and he can read in the garden."

"We'll be here at two then," said Emma.

* * *

At two o'clock, Emma brought Alain to Ana's consultation room. Then she walked outside to enjoy the garden, as much as she could, knowing what was coming.

Alain settled into the rocking chair.

"How have you been getting along since you got home, Alain?"

"I'm doing fine. Just a little jumpy when I hear noises in the street or when someone knocks at the door."

"I've asked you to come here today to talk about a very delicate subject. I've tried to think of ways to ask you about this, but I've ultimately decided that the best way is just to come out and ask you. Okay?"

"Okay."

"This man who kidnapped you and told you he was your father, did he ever make any sexual advances toward you?"

"You mean did he try to molest me sexually?"

"Yes, that's what I want to know."

"Absolutely not."

"Do you know what sexual molestation is?"

"Yes, I have been warned about strangers trying to do things to young people. My mother, my aunt Marguerite, my grandmother, Reyna, and my grandfather, and even my father warned me about those kinds of people. If one person is attracted to another or in love with them, then sex is okay. And that was what I was taught. And the sex of the person doesn't matter. Otherwise, it's a no, no."

Ana smiled, and moved on to other questions. "I know Maurice drugged you. Did you feel sore in any of your private parts when you became conscious?"

"No. If he had tried to molest me, I would have woken up. Believe me, that man did a bad thing by kidnapping me, but he didn't do anything of the kind you're asking about. He never took my clothes off."

"I'm satisfied it didn't happen, Alain, thank you for coming in to talk with me about this. Your knowledge and your clarity are very helpful."

"When people I don't know try to touch me, I don't like it."

"I understand very well. You are safe here, Alain. That's what counts. Can you ask your mother to come in? I see she gave you a book to read, what is it?"

"She didn't give it to me, I told you about this book. It's *Robinson Crusoe.*"

"Ah yes, the adventure story you told me about that helped you survive."

* * *

Emma enjoyed the calmness of Ana's garden, daydreaming about her life in Paris.

She remembered sitting and looking out a window of the apartment that she shared with her friend Marguerite and Marguerite's mother, Reyna. It overlooked the Seine River. She was still a young woman and had lost all the weight she gained during her pregnancy. She wore her blond hair pulled back and tied with a bright colored ribbon. She was at peace. Motherhood agreed with her.

She was watching Alain, who was then four years old, walk down the Quai des Grand Augustins hand-in-hand in the bright afternoon with Marguerite. She was in the sunlit living room filled with portraits she had painted over the years, carefully chosen so they would pick up the colors from the multi-toned Moroccan carpets spread over the floor. She saw that Alain and Marguerite were deeply engaged in conversation, and she could almost hear Marguerite telling him of an adventure she had had as a reporter, or one of the tales from the Arabian Nights. Marguerite had a rich imagination, and Alain was an insatiable audience. Emma's thoughts were interrupted by Reyna, who came into the room.

Reyna said that Marguerite loved Alain as if he were her own child, and that Reyna herself loved him more than her own life. She said he was probably the only grandchild she would ever have.

Emma was basking in the warmth of her good fortune. She and Marguerite had been together for almost five years. It was a totally unexpected relationship, but it had worked out beyond her imagination. It started a few months after Ian disappeared and Marguerite and her mother had taken her in. They had installed her in the room that she and Marguerite now shared.

On a very special evening while she was pregnant, Emma had just come back from school carrying the weariness from the extra weight the baby added to her body. She struggled up the one flight of stairs, but she was thankful she didn't have to climb the four flights to reach her old apartment. As usual, the hot mint tea and the delicacies were ready. Reyna greeted her affectionately with one of the few colloquial Arabic sayings Emma could understand, "Did you have a busy day, Laziza?"

Emma had answered absentmindedly, "Yes, very full and very busy," and remembered thinking, it would be impossible to explain to anyone what this atmosphere meant to her mental state. At school, she was engaged in art, which filled her with satisfaction, yet coming home to the kind of ambiance this family provided her, truly made her life exceptional. It was also important because she was deeply hurt by her father's rejection of her when she told him of her pregnancy. He stopped communicating with her once he learned of it. Emma felt like a big fat elephant, but she had never been more content.

Emma rested until dinner, chatting with Reyna about the day's activities. Marguerite arrived about six-thirty from her desk at the international news agency where she worked as one of their top reporters. She was highly valued there, and three other agencies were after her to work for them because she had a keen understanding of Middle East politics. Since she spoke all the languages of the region, she was worth her weight in gold. She was also on top of the French national scene, which she followed with great interest, even while in Algeria.

Marguerite always put out her Gauloises on the flat landing, knowing that the smoke would make Emma sick, but the smell lingered on her. When she entered the flat, she kissed both her mother and Emma on the cheeks. Her aperitif was already poured and the three of them lounged near the fireplace, Reyna and Emma drinking mint tea, and Marguerite sipping her Campari.

Marguerite asked her mother what she was cooking as she removed her smartly tailored black jacket of Thai silk and her brightly colored Hermes scarf and placed them on the back of the nearest chair.

"Tuna," was Reyna's quick reply.

"My favorite," she said. "I could smell the cayenne when I walked through the kitchen."

"Dinner is served," announced Reyna.

The three of them sat at the table. As they dined, the conversation drifted towards Emma.

Reyna noted that Emma was having difficulty getting around.

Emma told her that she was quite uncomfortable. She couldn't see the tips of her toes, and felt like she was carrying a big sack of potatoes. She talked about how busy her baby was, as it wouldn't stop kicking her. Emma said again that she was very happy to be pregnant, but she was exhausted.

"The next two months will be hell," Reyna followed up. "You should ask for time off from school."

It was very near the end of the term, Emma told her, so she could manage. She only had two more projects to do, anyway, and she just didn't want to get depressed.

Marguerite told her that she and Reyna would keep Emma's spirits up. Marguerite told Emma to go to her bed and rest. She would have a cigarette and come and give her a massage.

Emma saw her standing outside on the balcony. The evening lights of Paris reflected off the river and gave off a glow that was irreplaceable. She could see Marguerite draw deeply on her Gauloises and wondered what she was doing out there for so long. Marguerite smoked two more cigarettes, then came back inside and went to the kitchen. Emma heard the kettle whistle, and a short time later, Marguerite came in with a basin of hot water and two towels on her arm. As she pushed the door open with her foot, the soft light made her thin and elegant form glow. Comparing her own awkward size, Emma's spirits crashed.

Marguerite asked her what was wrong.

Emma said she felt big and awkward and told Marguerite it was hard to get around.

Marguerite told her she had something that would help. She took off Emma's slippers, soaked one of the towels in the piping hot water, squeezed it, flapped it momentarily in the air, and then wrapped Emma's foot in it. She repeated the exercise with the other towel on her right foot. Then she rubbed her bulging tummy, and Emma started to relax and some of her humor returned.

Emma began to stroke Marguerite's head, grateful and full of affection for her. Marguerite lay down beside her on the bed and kissed her softly. Emma did not resist. She had come to love Marguerite. She received Marguerite's tongue and kept stroking her head. Emma knew they had a deep connection almost from their first meeting. After Emma moved in with Marguerite and her mother, she had expected this advance and had thought the only reason it hadn't happened before was because of her pregnancy.

Emma kissed her in return, searching out her tongue and pushing hard against it. Marguerite opened Emma's robe and began to lick her extended belly, and then moved to her enlarged breasts, kissing and biting the nipples. Emma felt a stirring deep inside her womb in a secret place never awakened before, and she started groaning. Marguerite caressed Emma's sex with her fingers and then with the tip of her tongue. Emma enjoyed the pleasure her friend was giving her and felt grateful for being desired, even though she was seven months pregnant. She began to tremble, and Marguerite looked up.

Emma whispered for her not to stop.

Marguerite was again beside her with her tongue in Emma's mouth, and her fingers were very gently stimulating Emma's sex to the point that Emma felt more aroused than she ever had been. Reaching a crescendo, she shuddered. Every muscle in her body contracted as she began to have an orgasm so complete and so fulfilling that she couldn't speak.

Slowly the contractions lessened. Her muscles relaxed, and she hugged and kissed Marguerite. She said, "Thank you, my love. Thank you, my love. You are my love."

The last two months of Emma's pregnancy, which would have otherwise been hell, were made happy by her new physical connection with Marguerite. She wondered if a man would have watched her body become so disfigured and done what her friend had done—made her feel so desirable and so whole. Emma thought it was remarkable that in this period she was able to experience her sexuality more fully than ever before in her life. This new love made her feel totally safe, and she opened up to Marguerite as to no other person in the world.

* * *

Emma walked through Ana's French door into her consultation room and took a seat in the same chair that Alain had just left. It was still moving back and forth a little from his departure. "Thank you for seeing me, Ana. How did it go with Alain?"

"It was exactly as you said, Emma. Maurice didn't touch him sexually. Alain was very straightforward about that. And now I am very clear, too. I only have one question for you. After he got home, did he complain about any soreness or pain in his private parts?"

"No, he didn't. If he had, I would have spoken immediately to the police about it. But now that this is out of the way, as I knew it would be, I needed to come back so I could talk something over with you, Ana. You know that I am French, and I came here from Paris where I lived for several years while I was going to school. I wanted you to know about my life there, especially about my love life." She then explained the tender memories she had been reliving in the garden.

Ana nodded. "I understand what you are saying, Emma."

"I wanted you to know about Marguerite because I need to explore the loss of that relationship and how it has affected my life."

"We will deal with that in good time, Emma. Thank you for sharing you life in Paris with me."

17

No Low-Hanging Fruit

SAMUEL WAS SITTING behind the two-way mirror while the chief of police, the district attorney, and Bernardi met with Sergeant Patruski. Even though he knew about the two-way mirror, Patruski had no idea that Samuel was there that day, watching and listening.

Bernardi had called the meeting because it was time to take a statement from Tony Patruski, the sergeant's son, and the father would not allow investigators to approach the boy directly. Bernardi had already checked on Patruski's background, including the FBI, and he had found some disturbing information that had been withheld by the officer when he joined the SFPD. Samuel thought the officer was protecting his son, or, even worse, that Patruski himself might be responsible for the killings.

Samuel had even convinced Mac that he needed to find out what make tire had run though the human excrement. After a lengthy investigation Mac had determined that it came from a Volkswagen bus. Since Maurice's 1960 bus was impounded they had tested the treads on its tires and found they didn't match the one at the murder scene. Patruski knew nothing of this finding. It was not necessary to disclose this information to him because it was a homicide matter, outside his jurisdiction.

The chief of police wasn't that cynical about Patruski's behavior. All he wanted to know was why one of his officers was preventing access to a witness. The district attorney wanted to know what the evidence was that linked the two murders to Maurice. If there was none, or if it was insufficient to convict him, he didn't want to proceed to trial against him.

He started the discussion. "Sergeant, I've been advised that you're preventing access to your son as a witness to events that may be important in a murder investigation. Is that true?"

"No, sir. We have the man who committed the murders. As far as I'm concerned, the case is closed."

"What do you say to that, Lieutenant Bernardi?"

"With all due respect to the sergeant, sir. We're looking for a suspect who molested the two boys before he shot them. We're not convinced that these murders are related to the kidnapping of Alain Sheridan. Maurice Levantine claimed that Alain Sheridan is his illegitimate son. He had some kind of relationship with the boy's mother before he was born. He believes that he is, and this claim gives him a motivation to kidnap the boy. That's far removed from the brutality of a murderer. Besides, Alain Sheridan made no claim of being molested or even held at gunpoint."

Samuel watched Patruski stand up looking insulted. "How in the hell would he have known? He was drugged!" he shouted. "And why would the bastard need to use a gun on him if the boy was in that condition?"

"Calm down, man," said the chief. "If we're accusing the wrong man, the real killer or killers are still out there and they could strike again. Our job is to see if we have the right one in jail."

"The boy had no physical signs of that kind of abuse," said Bernardi.

"Look. I know that Maurice bastard did it. Everything points to him," said Patruski, spittle shooting from his mouth as he shouted. "And, I hope you notice that there haven't been any more kidnapping or murders since he was arrested."

"Let me go in another direction, sergeant. Your son was a good friend of both murdered boys, wasn't he?" asked Bernardi.

"What's that got to do with anything?" snarled Patruski.

"That's why we're here today, sergeant," said Bernardi. "We need to talk with him to find out more about them and him too."

Samuel watched as Patruski's eyes narrowed, and he wiped his hands on his pants legs as if they were wet with sweat. "I'm not giving my son up for some bullshit conspiracy theory."

Samuel, who was behind the two-way mirror, could see the stress on Patruski's face as he fended off the chief and Bernardi. It looked to him like they were closing in on him the way hunters do to a trapped animal.

"We understood he had sleepovers with at least one of the murdered boys, so we're assuming that they were pretty close friends," said Bernardi. "That's the truth, isn't it?"

"But the rest of the crap about him isn't."

"Tell us what you mean," said the chief.

"There's been a lot of bullshit talk about my son, that's all," he said. Samuel noted that he was really trying to restrain himself, but there was a twitching of his left eyelid that he couldn't control.

"Did he ever talk to you about his sleepovers with … Phillip, I believe was the boy's name?"

"He said they watched a lot of movies."

"At whose house?"

"At Phillip's."

"What did they do at your house?"

"They'd go down to Geary Street and get pizzas and some cokes."

"Did they both sleep in the same room at your house?"

"Yes, Anthony has a bedroom with bunk beds in it."

"Did you ever see them sleeping in the same bed together?"

Samuel saw Patruski trying to hold himself together, but with that question, he finally broke. "He's not a queer, goddamn it, and I won't let anyone accuse him of that!"

Samuel thought he looked like a defenseless child who had just been accused of robbing his own piggy bank. He collapsed, setting his head on his folded arms. It was hard not to feel sorry for him.

Samuel watched while the room went quiet for a moment. Then he saw Bernardi get up and put his arm around the slouched figure to comfort him. He said softy, "We're not out to accuse him of anything, sergeant. We know your wife committed suicide and that you've been raising him alone. Not an easy job for anyone, especially with her death and him discovering her body. We just want information. And we'll go as easy on him as you want us to, as long as we find out what he knows about those boys that might lead us to solving this case."

Samuel watched carefully what was going on in the room with a sense of skepticism. What he had learned of Patruski's past behavior was hard to reconcile with the man who had dissolved into a bowl of trembling jello at the interrogation table, but there still wasn't enough evidence to make him an actual suspect, so he hoped that Bernardi wouldn't bring up what he had learned about Patruski from his days in Chicago. It was probably enough to get him fired if it could be proved, but they still didn't know if he had used violence, and if so, to what extent.

Patruski took a handkerchief out of his pocket, and wiped his brow. "All right, I'll let you talk to him, but I want to be present."

"I don't think that's a good idea," said Bernardi. "He's not going to be frank with us if you're there. We'll give you a transcript of what he says, as long as you agree not to discipline him too severely for what he tells us. Of course, if he implicates himself in a crime, it's an entirely different matter."

"I'll tell you what," said Patruski, regaining his composure, as he sat up straight as a rod. "I'll bring him in tomorrow morning—how's that? Who do you want him to meet with?"

"Lieutenant Bernardi can take a statement from him. That will be fine," said the chief. "But I want it understood that he's going to tell us all he knows."

"I'll tell him that is what you want from him," said Patruski, as he got up and left, pushing rudely by Bernardi.

* * *

Back in Bernardi's office, Samuel was pacing the floor. "I hope you didn't fall for that line of bullshit he was giving you."

"Let's not jump to any conclusions because of what you found out in Chicago. We still have to verify it, and it seems to have had more to do with the petty crap that goes on in big city departments. The question will be if there was serious harm done to people."

"What are you talking about?" said Samuel. "What happens in big city departments when cops go around collecting money for protection, and the people who are supposed to pay can't, or won't?"

"Okay, I see what you mean, they get hurt, but it's not usually the cop that does the hurting. It's turned over to some low level thug. Besides, in fairness to Patruski, these are all rumors, yet to be proven."

"But there's enough to make us wonder if this guy is hiding more than his past," said Samuel.

"I grant you that. But let's not go overboard. Let's see

what his kid tells us."

"I wouldn't be surprised if he showed up with a lawyer, and we get nothing," said Samuel, pounding one fist into his palm. "Then there's the suicide of the wife. Why did she do it? Maybe Patruski was such a bastard to her that she just pulled the plug to get away from him," said Samuel.

"We investigated that when it happened," said Bernardi. "She was a profoundly depressed person, on medication, and had had several treatments of shock therapy. Can you imagine what it must have been like for the guy to try and hold his job, and raise a kid, and still take care of her? I felt sorry for him, just trying to cope. Didn't you see him this morning, shaking like a leaf?"

"I have my own take on that performance," said Samuel. "What do we actually know about this kid?"

"Not much, Patruski has kept us at arm's length."

"I can't get any information from his schools, but you can," said Samuel.

"Okay, I'll try, but I don't think I can get it done today. I also doubt if he'll admit to anything when we talk with him tomorrow. Do you really think he could be a suspect in these murders?"

"I don't know what to think," said Samuel. "All I know is his dad has kept us away from him and keeps pushing for the DA to try an innocent man for murder. We don't have anywhere else to go. So let's start over with Tony, and let's see where it goes."

* * *

The next morning Tony Patruski showed up at the interrogation room with Hiram Goldberg, a jowly defense attorney with black curly hair, stiff white starched collar, and gold bracelets. Samuel knew him quite well from having seen him on previous cases. He had represented his friend Rafael Garcia in his first case, the one involving the Chinese jars. Then he showed up again to represent Dusty Schwartz, the tortured dwarf. He was very smart and very quick and not likely to allow his client to say anything meaningful.

Hiram sat opposite the two-way mirror and opened his briefcase in front of Tony who was sitting next to him. They were both facing Samuel. Bernardi and the assistant district attorney were already sitting at the table with their backs to Samuel, so neither Tony nor his lawyer could occupy that space. Samuel knew that Hiram suspected he was behind the mirror, and he wanted to frustrate the reporter's study of his client's body language. Bernardi turned on the tape recorder.

"My name is Hiram Goldberg," he announced, and shook hands with Bernardi and the assistant district attorney. "I'm here with Anthony Patruski so he can answer your questions. Let me say this in preparation of what's going to happen here." Tony was a pale boy who looked his stated age of thirteen. He had dark hair that was cut short. His face was thin, and his brown eyes were set deep in his sockets. He acted upset, and his movements were jerky.

"Tony has been through quite a lot in the past few months, in losing two dear friends, and in the past few years losing his mother as well, so he hopes that your questions will honor his delicate state of mind." He smiled slightly at Bernardi and the assistant DA and winked at the two-way mirror.

"Thank you Mr. Goldberg, it's nice to see you again. You look prosperous and well, as usual. I would like to give your client some precautions, if you don't mind. He needs to answer my questions out loud. No gestures or mumbles. If he doesn't hear or understand a question, please have him tell me, and I will try and make it clearer. I don't want you to guess at any answer. If he doesn't know an answer, he needs to say he doesn't know. Do we understand each other so far?"

Hiram gestured for Tony to answer.

"Yeah," said Tony.

"First, I have to swear you in. Do you promise to tell the truth, the whole truth, and nothing but the truth, so help you God."

"Yeah. I do."

"You're thirteen years old. Am I correct?

"Yeah."

"And you're in the sixth grade at Towne School."

"Yeah, so what."

"So you're behind your grade level?"

"That's right. I'm working on it."

"We understand that you were friends with the two boys who were killed?"

"Yeah. I was closer to Phillip Atkinson than I was to Bruce Axelrod."

"Did you pal around with them at school?"

"Yeah."

"What about after school?"

"Not so much with Bruce but definitely with Phillip. But Bruce hooked up with Phil and me a few weeks before his death. He wanted to be closer to Phil for some reason."

"Did he ever say why?"

"Not to me."

"How about overnights?"

"Yeah, Phil and I would have sleepovers at my house and at his sometimes."

"What would you two do at these sleepovers?"

Hiram stood up and jangled his gold bracelets, looking first at the two-way mirror, and then at Bernardi. "Hold on, lieutenant, I want my client to answer your question, but I want you to ask a better question. This one is too general. If you find out later that he left something out, you'll accuse him of lying."

Samuel noted that Tony looked angry.

"Fair enough, Mr. Goldberg. Can you tell me first in general what you two would do at an overnight?"

"Philip had a movie theatre in his home. His father built it, and it had a fancy projector. We would go to Papa's pizza place on Geary and then to his house, and he would load one of the movies into the fancy projector, and we would watch it. At some point we would dig into the pizza and drink cokes."

"What kind of movies would you see?"

"Usually horror films, if we could find one that we hadn't seen."

"Where did his father get them?"

"I guess he bought them. You really have to ask him."

"Were those the only films that you saw? The ones he had at his home?"

"Yeah."

"Can you give me the names of some of them?"

"The one we liked the best was *Night of the Living Dead.* But we also watched all of the Frankenstein flicks that we could find and all of the werewolf ones with Lon Chaney, Jr. We were both big fans of Bela Lugosi, and we couldn't get enough of him. He was our hero."

"Did you watch any other kind of films?"

At this question, Samuel noted that Tony started to squirm in his seat.

Hiram stood up again. "Just a minute, lieutenant," he smiled. "You have to be specific, so we know what you're asking."

"Did you watch any pornographic films?"

"Nah."

"Very well. Have you ever seen any pornography?"

Hiram jumped to his feet, again, "My client doesn't have to answer that question. That's an invasion of privacy, and it's irrelevant."

Samuel saw that each time Hiram took over, Tony relaxed, as if he could avoid answering or was given a hint what to say.

"A harmless question, Mr. Goldberg, I assume all boys take a look at pornography at some time in their youth."

"At thirteen years old? Give me a break."

"Did you and Phillip look through any magazines?"

"We did see a *Playboy* magazine when my father forgot to lock it up."

"How many times?"

"Only once. The next time Phil was over at my house, the cabinet was locked. That was it."

"Did you and Phillip ever sleep in the same bed?"

Again, the boy blanched, but then looked straight at Bernardi and answered. "No."

It was obvious to Samuel that Tony was increasingly nervous at the line of questioning, and was lying. He twitched again and his jerky movements increased.

"Did Phillip ever tell you that he had sex with another boy?"

"No!"

"Did he ever tell you that he had sex with anyone?"

"No."

"Did you and he ever talk about sex?"

"We did talk about nice behinds and nice breasts on older girls we knew. And that one time we saw *Playboy*. That was all."

"Did Phillip ever make a pass at you?"

"Of course not!"

"Did you ever make a pass at Phillip?"

Hiram was on his feet again. This time looking directly at the two-way mirror. "Are you trying to ruin this boy's life? Once this kind of talk is on the table, even if it's false, it can't be taken back. I am telling you right now, this boy is not a queer."

"I never made a pass at Phillip, and he never made a pass at me!" the boy exclaimed, very upset. "I am not a queer, and this stuff never came up between us, or for that matter with Bruce Axelrod either."

"We have information that you told your classmates that they could stop worrying because the killer had been caught. We assume you got that information from you father, is that correct?"

"Yeah, that's what he told me."

"Who did he say it was?"

"He said it was a French guy named Maurice Levantine."

"Did you know Mr. Levantine?"

"Never heard of him until my father mentioned his name. He told me that he had been caught for kidnapping another boy around our age."

"Did he tell you any of the evidence he had to prove that it was him?"

"No. He's in charge of kidnapping cases. He knew what he was talking about. He doesn't usually talk with me about those cases."

"Really?" Bernardi's eyebrow shot up.

"Really. He told me because he knew we were all scared that it might happen to us, and he wanted us to know that they caught the guy."

"Does your father smoke cigarettes?"

"He did until my mother died, but then he quit."

"Do you ever smoke cigarettes?"

"Yeah. I smoke once in a while. So what."

"Did you share them with Phillip?"

"Nah. He didn't like them."

"Do you smoke dope?"

"No."

"Did you ever smoke dope?"

"Just a minute, lieutenant. That's against the law. This boy doesn't have to answer that kind of question," said Hiram.

"Did either of your friends, Phillip or Bruce, ever smoke dope with you?"

Again, Hiram interrupted. "Don't answer that question."

"Were you ever with either of them when they smoked dope?"

"Nah."

"Let me ask you this, Tony. You've been pretty arrogant here today. Do you think that because your dad is a cop that you don't have to cooperate with us?"

"Don't answer that question, it's argumentative, and you're badgering the witness," said the lawyer.

"Let the record reflect that Tony Patruski didn't answer my last question, but now has a smirk on his face. That's all the questions I have for you right now. Obviously, I'll have more for you when you change your attitude and show a willingness to help us get to the bottom of this mess. You're not off the hook yet, Mr. Patruski."

Hiram closed his briefcase and winked again at the two-way mirror. Tony Patruski nodded. He got up and left the room followed by his attorney. On his way out he yelled, "Wait until I tell my dad the crappy way you treated me."

Once they were gone, Samuel went into the interrogation room. "You didn't get much from that arrogant little shit," he said. "We can get the list of what they watched from Phillip's parents, but if they weren't watching porn, he would have let him answer the question in the negative. The question is where would they have gotten that kind of movie?"

Bernardi was thoughtful for a moment. "He's a couple of years older than the other boys. He was probably a negative influence on both of them. How can we find out how things were with his father after his mother died? Do we know if he went to some kind of counseling, and if he did, how am I going to get my hands on the doctor's notes?"

"Almost impossible, unless the father agrees to the doctor releasing them," said Samuel. "But I bet you have some informants running around the Geary Street dives that can give us some information on whether or not these boys bought pizza at Papa's or got adults to buy them liquor or marijuana."

"What about him being in trouble with the law? Any record?"

The assistant DA spoke for the first time. "I studied the files last night. His father probably protected him from having any kind of a record, as you heard him say on the way out. He certainly thinks the rules don't apply to him."

"You didn't get much in the way of evidence that would point to either of the Patruskis as suspects. I think you need a new approach to this. There's no low-hanging fruit that we can get our hands on."

"I agree with you," said Samuel, "that's why I'm going back to talk with the teacher."

"Can you ask her if she saw any signs of the kind of behavior we saw here today?"

"I'll make a point of it," said Samuel.

18

Oh, No!

Early the next morning Samuel got two phone calls within minutes of one another. The first was his bird dog, who monitored the police calls. The second was Bernardi. "There's been another kidnapping and murder of a young boy. I'll pick you up in twenty minutes, so we can go to the alleyway where it happened."

Samuel was sitting propped up on a pillow in his bed in shorts and a T-shirt, rubbing the sleep out of his eyes. "I know. I just got the word from my man. I'll be ready when you get here."

"That's not all. Tony Patruski ran away from home last night, and he stole his father's gun."

"Wow! You think he killed the kidnapped boy?" asked Samuel.

"Too early to tell. But I doubt it. He would have to have gotten the boy to the same alleyway where the others were killed. He's only thirteen years old, and I don't think he knows how to drive, or even has access to a car."

"I think you're right. That kid isn't a murderer. He's just a lost boy in my opinion. But I'm not so sure about this dad."

"Let's wait and see where the facts lead us," said Bernardi.

Samuel jumped out of bed and into the shower and was ready a few minutes later when Bernardi picked him up. They drove to the South of Market area where the previous killings had taken place. As they were approaching the scene they heard the sirens screaming and the lights blazing from the patrol cars.

At the end of the small alleyway there were various police officers from homicide plus Mac, the forensic tech, and the medical examiner, Barney McLeod. Both he and Mac escorted Bernardi and Samuel down the alleyway to where the young boy's body was located next to the brick wall at the end. The boy had been shot in the head like the other two, but this time Mac had collected the parts of the shattered bullet that had been initially ignored in one of the other murders. Samuel saw the body lying in a pool of blood with the back of his head blown off. He had never seen such a mess.

"Is it possible all that blood is his?" he asked the crowd around him.

Turtle Face, the medical examiner, answered his question. "Yes, it's his all right. If he hadn't died of the head wound, he would have bled to death.

"That's not all," said Turtle Face, "we also found and saved the pile of human excrement that we expected to find in this string of killings. It looks like the same nut did this one as all the others, unless he has an evil twin."

"We need to catch whoever committed these murders, fast," said Samuel, "instead of worrying about defending Maurice and wasting our time with Patruski's nonsense."

"I agree," said Bernardi. "We have an all-points bulletin out for Patruski's son. If we can get our hands on that gun, we can zero in on one of them or eliminate both father and son."

"I think the boy ran away because he was ashamed of being accused of being queer. In my opinion he was just experimenting as most young boys do. I'm less sure about the motivations of the father. It's certainly disconcerting that the boy disappeared last night though."

"By the way, where is Patruski this morning?" asked Bernardi.

"I bet he's out looking for his son, just as any parent would, and just as I did when Alain went missing. You can't blame him for that, especially since the boy is obviously a disaster, and maybe the father too."

"Or a maniacal serial killer," said Bernardi, "as you have previously suggested."

After an hour at the scene, it was pretty clear to both Bernardi and Samuel that this was the work of the same person who committed the previous murders. All that was missing was the rambling ransom note that they expected would be in the mail in the next couple of days. The medical examiner removed the body.

This time there were no tire tracks in the pile of excrement.

* * *

Back in the office, Samuel and Bernardi were sitting at his small conference table.

"Was this boy from the same school as the others?" Samuel asked.

"No, he apparently lived in the Marina. So far it seems that he didn't have any connection with the other boys. I will visit his parents as soon as they're able to talk."

"I'd like to go with you, but that's very sensitive. The best thing I can do right now is go and talk to the teacher again," said Samuel.

Just as he was ready to leave, the phone rang. It was Sergeant Patruski. His son had been caught in the main rail yard of downtown Los Angeles and was taken into custody by the railroad detectives, and then turned over to the police department. He had the gun with him, and he was being held in juvenile hall. His father had taken a PSA flight to Los Angeles and was with him. As Samuel had suspected, he said he fled because the issue of his sexuality had come up, and he felt deeply ashamed that it had been made public. He assured his father that he and Phillip had only experimented with sex and that he was not queer as the police had insinuated in their interrogation of him.

After Patruski hung up, Bernardi talked with the investigator in charge of the boy's case. He asked that the gun be forwarded to him directly as it was necessary to send it to ballistics. Patruski had asked that it be turned over to him as it was his, but the authorities told Bernardi that they would first test it to see if it was involved in any crimes in the L.A. area. If not, it would be sent directly to Bernardi in San Francisco. When asked why he took the gun, the boy said it was for self-protection, he had no intention of using it to commit a crime.

"You realize we're not even close to solving these cimes," said Samuel, "but we need to know where Patruski was last night without tipping him off that we want to investigate his involvement."

"The first thing I have to do is examine his gun. The investigator told me it's a snub-nosed .38 revolver, like the one that was used in the killings, but we need to test it to see if it fired any of the bullets, or remnants we've reconstructed."

"How long do you think it will take to get it here?" asked Samuel.

"No more than a few days."

With that Samuel went to keep his appointment with Miss Jensen, the teacher.

19

Emma's Talk with Ana

As Samuel made his way to see the teacher, Emma kept her appointment with Ana. She walked through Ana's lovely garden into the room with the rocking chairs. When they were comfortably seated across from each other, Ana asked, "What would you like to talk about today, Emma?"

"I would like you to know how my relationship with Marguerite ended."

Ana could tell how distressed she was by the pained look on her face. "I'm here to listen," she said.

"When Marguerite came back from an assignment to the Golan Heights with a terrible cough, she tried to convince me and her mother that she was just worn down by the intensity of what she had been through. But the cough didn't get any better, so we insisted that she go to the doctor. The news wasn't good. She had lung cancer. The treatment was brutal. Because she was a heavy smoker, the doctor was not surprised that it had attacked someone as young as Marguerite. At first, she and I cried together and held each other. To some extent we were both in denial about the significance of the disease.

"Marguerite worried for her mother Reyna, while I worried for Alain because he was so attached to his tante, as he called her, and she to him. Neither one of us could bear to tell the boy anything, but he knew something was happening. He could sense the tension in the air. The stress showed on his young face, and he started wetting the bed again.

"Once, when Marguerite's treatment was just beginning, he came to our room, brushed his dark hair aside, and looked her over closely.

"'What's wrong with you, tante Marguerite?' he asked.

"'Nothing, my little one,' she answered. 'Why would you think that?'

"He told her that she looked very pale, and she made strange noises when she breathed.

"Marguerite tried to convince him that she was just very tired from her trip, and that when she had rest she would feel fine again. But Alain knew better, so he came to me.

"'Tante Marguerite is very sick, isn't she, Maman?'

"I took him out of the bedroom because I decided that I couldn't lie to him any longer, and told him that she had a very serious lung disease.

"He saw tears in my eyes and asked if she was going to die.

"I told him we didn't know, that only time would tell, and we had to pray for her. I said we must be brave, just as she was being. If God was willing, she would recover, and we could go on with our lives.

"Alain was very scared. 'And if she doesn't, Maman, what will happen to me? Will you leave me, too?' His voice wobbled when he spoke.

"I assured him I would always be with him, and so would Marguerite, even if only in spirit, and that we would go through it together.

"Reyna was in the kitchen making an Algerian soup, listening to us. She was cutting celery, her feet planted firmly on the ground, as if she were preparing a meal in a tent in the desert. Her thick black hair was pulled straight back, and she had an apron bound tightly around her plump midsection when I entered the room with Alain.

"She told me that Marguerite would probably not live, and that since her husband died Marguerite was all she had in the world. She knew from the time her daughter was very young that she was not an ordinary person and would never marry. That is why Reyna was so happy when she made friends with me and brought me home. Reyna was even happier when Alain was born. We gave her a family that she could take care of, and a happy life, and now the three of us had to stick together and give Marguerite all the comfort we could."

Emma paused, lost in her sad memories.

"Would you like a cup of jasmine tea?" offered Ana

"Let me get through this part of it first," answered Emma with a strained smile.

"We agreed that we would unite our thoughts and prayers and hoped things would get better, but that did not happen. I went with Marguerite to the doctor, and I was there when he told her he was going to have to take out part of her right lung. He was clear with her. He didn't make any promises.

"Marguerite didn't lose any of her sense of humor or her affection for our small family. She had a different view of the whole thing, as she explained to me, after we left the doctor's office.

"'I did not come into the world to make others suffer because of my weaknesses,' she said.

"I told her not to be silly, that her condition was not a weakness, it was an illness that could be treated.

"But she didn't think so. She said she knew her body, and this thing has got her, and she wouldn't be able to defeat it. So, she would have to face it. And she wanted me to face it too, because when she went, I would have to take care of her mother. She told me that I was like a daughter to Reyna—the only one that she would have left.

"Tears streamed down my cheeks as I tried to deal with this new reality, but I wasn't ready to give up. I had many long conversations with my father who had lived and worked in the coal-mining region of the country and had several friends with black lung disease. He had countless stories of people overcoming incredible deprivations and illnesses during the war. I always hung up the telephone encouraged and convinced that we would win the battle and that my friend would live out her days with us. I tried to pass this certainty on to Marguerite, but she only smiled and patted me on a shoulder, always on her way to doing other things.

"Marguerite had the operation and healed nicely. She even stopped coughing for a while. The awful greenish shade of her skin faded, and it returned to an almost normal color. The four of us could now walk arm in arm by the river on Sundays as we used to. I hoped desperately that Marguerite was on the road to recovery, and I tried to convince myself that it was time to stop worrying.

"'God, please, keep Marguerite safe,' I prayed daily.

"Reyna prayed, 'God, please don't let her suffer too much.'"

* * *

Emma drank her jasmine tea slowly. She thought about coming back another day, but she wanted to finish the story she was telling Ana.

"I was sitting by the window. The sun came in through the winter clouds and splashed on the Moroccan carpet. I remember Marguerite sitting in that same room in a rocking chair with a blanket wrapped around her legs. It was very cold outside during her last weeks.

"We spent a lot of time alone, in silence, holding hands. Both of us knew that every minute was precious. Alain was at school during the day, and Reyna went daily to the market on Rue de Buci looking for herbs to brew a special tea they both hoped would ease Marguerite's pain. The doctor had given her two weeks to live; she inhaled with a rattle and could no longer walk. Her skin color was gray, and sometimes, I couldn't feel her pulse.

"The doctor came three times a day to give her a shot of morphine, but he wouldn't give us any extra to use when he was not available. For the first week and a half, we accepted that, but soon her mother and I decided it was ridiculous to let her suffer so needlessly. We consulted Algerian friends who provided us with more than an adequate supply to keep our beloved with us for as long as possible without too much pain.

"I am afraid of death. It is a shadow that has lurked over me since birth, when my mother died. Death was the enemy, and I would do anything to avoid it, but Reyna and Marguerite taught me otherwise. They accepted it naturally, as a continuum of life, as another dimension of reality.

"One day when I sat in the same room doing Marguerite's nails, another of the small rituals we had created to comfort each other, she pulled me closer and kissed me on the lips. The effort seemed too much for her as she fought for air, panting, with that terrible gravelly noise that accompanied almost every breath. I started crying with my head on my lover's pillow.

"'My mother will be with you and with Alain,' Marguerite managed to say.

"I tried to shush her. I couldn't stand the idea of her dying.

"'Don't be afraid, you will do just fine. You are strong,' said Marguerite.

"Something inside me made me lift my head. We looked each other in the eyes for a long moment, and suddenly the fear that had always been in my heart, casting a heavy black shadow, melted away, leaving me trembling and clean.

"'I know, Marguerite. You have taught me about strength,' I replied, and we both smiled.

"There were times when Marguerite asked not to be medicated because she wanted to be lucid. One such occasion was on an evening three days before her death. She called me to her side. I took her cold hands in mine and started to stroke them as I observed the pain in my lover's thin, bony face. As she spoke, Marguerite gasped for air.

"'I have a secret to tell you, Emma. I have held it inside for many years,' she wheezed, 'and it is time to confess it to you.'

"'What is it, Marguerite?' I asked. 'You can tell me anything, you know that.'

"Marguerite tried to laugh but could only cough as she struggled to breathe. 'My secret is shameful to me, but it is very important for you to know,' she explained.

"She talked for a long time, pausing to catch her breath when she coughed, while I listened, numbed by what she told me. Her speech was confused, and it took several minutes for what she was telling me to sink in. She had withheld several letters that Ian had sent me after he returned to America, telling me of his love for me.

"'I am very … very … sorry,' she said.

"I told her she shouldn't be, she had done it out of love for me. She explained that she just wanted to protect me and Alain, but she was also jealous.

"In the following days, I felt both anger and sadness, but I couldn't deal with it at that time, it would have to wait. Caring for Marguerite was all that mattered at that moment.

"On Sunday night, I phoned my father and asked him to come and help me, as Marguerite's death was very near. He arrived the next afternoon. Janus gave Reyna a recipe for a Polish tea that would ease Marguerite's journey to the other side. He said it was used to help wounded soldiers during the war when there was no hope and no other recourse. Reyna went off to see if she could buy the list of ingredients. When she returned with everything, she brewed the tea and helped her daughter sip it. Marguerite was grayer than I had ever seen her. We also gave her more morphine. At that point Janus took his grandson by the hand and left the house for a long walk by the river.

"Shortly after two in the afternoon she was gone. She died peacefully and quietly with her mother and me holding her. I was not sure, but it seemed to me there were many spirits in the room. Reyna was talking to her dead husband in French, and I could sense his presence as well. There was no music in the room, but it felt as if there were. We laid Marguerite out, closed her eyes, and washed her body, removing the green bile that had escaped from her mouth and sullied the sheets. Her mother tied a white scarf tightly around her head pulling up her chin so her mouth would remain closed.

"Reyna and I cried tears of deep sorrow and of great relief, as Marguerite's illness had been so painful and lasted so long. Reyna began to ululate with that high pitched staccato scream of grieving Arab women. She pulled at her hair as she crawled on the floor, calling her daughter's name and keeping up the repetition. I was stunned, not knowing how to comfort her. Suddenly the ululating stopped, as if all her strength were exhausted. A few minutes later she composed herself, put her hair back in place, and once again was calm and focused. Only the stream of tears betrayed her inconsolable grief.

"When my father and Alain came home, Marguerite was beautifully laid out with candles around her and dressed in white. The boy knew she had died. He didn't say anything. He grabbed my hand and brought me over to Reyna and held us both very tightly.

"'This means she will never come back, doesn't it, Mama?' Alain asked.

"'It means she will not be with us physically,' I replied.

"Because his aunt had been sick for so long, he seemed to understand that her illness had killed her, and that did not mean I was going to leave him as well. I thought he had come to terms with that, but only time would tell.

"My father took care of the funeral arrangements. His large presence brought comfort to us, the two women, and to his little grandson.

"We had a moving ceremony at the church where Alain was baptized, simple and elegant as Marguerite would have liked. We buried her beside her father, General Henri, on a cold winter day.

"My grief was paralyzing, and I had difficulty moving. I could barely take care of Alain, so Reyna did it. She was sad but resigned because she never doubted that she would meet her daughter again in another life where they would both be with her husband. I cried for the loss of Marguerite, my friend, my lover, my sister. We had been together for what seemed a lifetime, and she had helped raise Alain and had given me a mother. At the same time, I realized I was also grieving the loss of Ian, although I didn't understand those feelings. I thought I had buried the memory of him years before, when I accepted the fact that he'd abandoned me."

* * *

Emma continued sitting in the rocking chair opposite the therapist sipping her jasmine tea and chatted happily about the progress Alain was making after he was returned home from being kidnapped.

"To me, he seems to have opened up, Ana."

"He still has some obstacles ahead of him. Please let me see him for another six months, at least. I have some things I want him to try, and I do believe he trusts me enough to help put some of my ideas for him into action. Is that what you wanted to talk to me about?"

"No. I will bring him to you, as you request, but I want you to know that this is my last session with you. Before I go, I want to talk with you about Ian.

"After Marguerite died, I was invited to San Francisco to exhibit my work, and I got in touch with Ian to let him know I was coming."

"Tell me about the feelings you had getting back in touch with Ian?"

"I was very hurt and angry with him. I loved him and hated him at the same time. When I found out that he had been trying to find me, and that Marguerite had hidden his letters from me, I was moved and grateful, since I felt that I had a lot of unfinished business with him. Besides, he was the father of my only child."

"I bet he was surprised to hear from you."

"Yes, he was, and happy too. He got to meet Alain and was very moved by knowing he had a son. I also told him that Marguerite had hidden his letters from me, so I didn't even know he was trying to find me.

"Our first meetings were … awkward, I believe, is the word you use. But very soon we got back our affection for one another, and he invited me to come to San Francisco and live with him. I told him all about my relationship with Marguerite and her death, and how now I had Reyna living with Alain and me, and she was part of my family, and I had to bring her with me."

"How did that work out with him?"

"It went very well. When I came to the U.S. I thought he and I could start over where we left off, and I could resolve some of those feelings of loss. We were working on that, and after I was here for six months, we married. Soon after that, the accident happened that left me crippled.

"Then he was called up by the army because he had been a part of the Reserve Officers' Training Corps at the university and had had a deferment. He went to Vietnam and was killed in the war. Another loss for me among the many in my life, and I feel that we never finished. So here I am with an unfinished life."

Ana smiled, "You're right Emma, the search never ends. But the next phase in your life that is still unfinished, is with Alain. That will take some time and patience. And you're lucky. You have Reyna. And I am also here to help you."

20

Running out of Possibilities

IT WAS MID-AFTERNOON when Samuel got off the Clement Street bus at Twenty-eighth Avenue and went to Miss Jensen's flat. She received him warmly and offered him coffee and some cookies. He sat in the same big armchair where he'd sat on his previous visit and told her about the interrogation of Tony Patruski and how he disappeared that very night and was captured in Los Angeles the next day. He also explained that another boy had been abducted and murdered the same night Tony disappeared. Samuel told her he doubted that Tony had anything to do with the murder, and that running away was probably connected with the interrogation and his shame about being asked about his sexuality.

"I need some more help from you, Miss Jensen. There are so many unanswered questions in this investigation that I thought you could give us some insights, and maybe even some more leads."

"I'll be glad to help, if I can," she answered. "But I didn't hear about another boy being kidnapped or killed."

"It wasn't one of the boys from your school. He lived in the Marina District."

She had a drawn look on her face. "My God, what is the world coming to? There has to be a way to end all this."

"That's in part why I'm here. We were headed in the wrong direction, and I want to get us moving toward a solution. First, I need to ask you some questions about the tutor, Mr. Harbano. I couldn't locate him in Georgia where he apparently comes from. I have in my notes that you suggested I contact Charles Hancock and ask him what kind of a car Harbano drove."

She nodded. "My answer is the same."

"Is Charles Hancock still at Towne School?"

"Yes, I saw him there this morning."

"That's good to know. Makes my job easier," said Samuel with relief. "Let me ask you one more question. Was there any after-school activity that the murdered boys took part in that we don't know about?"

She thought for a moment. "Not an after-school program, but there was one for summer sports that I think some of the boys participated in. I personally don't know much about it, because it didn't have anything to do with the school. The deceased boys' parents may know something about it, or even Charles Hancock, if he was in it."

"This is the first I've heard of it," he said, with a look of surprise. "Do you know who runs it, or how I can get in touch with that person or persons?"

"I'm sorry, I don't. As I said, it has nothing to do with the school; it's a summer program. I just heard a student, Charles Hancock, talk about it in passing. I've never seen it in operation."

"Is that the same boy who called Phillip Atkinson a queer?"

"Yes, that's him."

"I have his address, and he's first on my list of boys to contact. In fact, that is where I'm going next. Can I use your phone to find out if he's at home? Better yet, do you mind calling on my behalf and telling him I'm on my way to see him now? That way he won't be so reluctant to talk to me."

Miss Jensen got on the phone and spoke to the boy's mother, paving the way for Samuel's visit. She hung up the phone and gave the V sign for victory to the reporter. "They're expecting you within the hour. They live on Sacramento Street, just before Park Presidio, right near the synagogue."

"Yes," smiled Samuel. "I have the address."

"If you take the Clement Street bus and get off at Arguello, you can walk the few blocks to their home."

"I have one more question before I leave. They took Tony Patruski's statement yesterday. He was very arrogant and very angry. Did you see any signs of that in school?

"To tell the truth, and since this is just between you and me, Tony probably didn't belong at Towne School. He was two years behind the rest of the boys, and he had trouble keeping up. Everyone knew he was only there because his dad was a big shot in the police department. He was a social hit though, so he didn't act out as arrogant or angry. If anything, he had an inferiority complex and would have done much better somewhere else. But he was stuck there for social reasons."

Samuel nodded. "I see. That makes sense to me. I want to thank you again, Miss Jensen. You've been really helpful." He shook her hand and left hurriedly so he could catch the next bus. On the way, he hoped that he could escape the feeling that he was running out of possibilities. He was worried that these crimes might never be solved.

* * *

The Hancock home was a spacious mansion in Pacific Heights. Samuel rang the bell and was met by a Filipino maid in a white uniform. "You must be Mr. Hamilton. Come in. Mrs. Hancock is expecting you." She led him into the parlor, a spacious room with bay windows overlooking the street. It was expensively furnished with Persian rugs and valuable Ming vases on fine seventeenth-century French tables. "Would you like a cup of tea or coffee or other refreshment?" she offered.

"No, thank you," he smiled, feeling out of place in his wrinkled khakis, sport coat, and penny loafers.

Mrs. Hancock entered the parlor from the upstairs and extended her hand to Samuel with a reserved smile. She was blond and elegantly coiffed and she wore a very chic blue silk print dress, but Samuel could smell alcohol over the expensive perfume she was wearing.

"Samuel Hamilton. Very nice meeting you, Mrs. Hancock."

"Marjorie," she said. "Oh Millie, did you offer Mr. Hamilton a drink?"

"Yes, Ma'am."

"Will you please bring me a glass of sherry?" asked Marjorie.

This relaxed Samuel a little. "I'm a reporter with the afternoon paper, and I'm investigating the deaths of a couple of students at Towne School, who were classmates of your son. And frankly, I'm looking for information. I've been helping Lieutenant Bernardi of the San Francisco Police Department. We're trying to come up with some solid leads, and I'm sorry to say that so far we haven't done so well."

"Really? My son told me something else. He said that the culprit was in jail."

"I don't mean to alarm you, but there has been another death, and it occurred while the supposed killer was in jail." Samuel noted that her eyes widened, and there was an apparent strain on her face. "Frankly, we never thought that the man jailed on an unrelated kidnapping charge had anything to do with the killings."

She started clasping her hands together with nervousness. Fortunately Millie arrived with Mrs. Hancock's drink just at that moment and handed it to her. "Are you sure you don't want something, Mr. Hamilton?" she asked, noticeably disturbed.

Samuel shook his head. He knew he had work to do and alcohol would only hinder him. "I was hoping I could ask your son some questions about the two boys. I'd like to get some kind of a background on them from a student's point of view."

"Certainly," she said. She got up from the plush sofa with a sense of urgency and called the maid. "Millie, ask Charles to come down and talk with us?"

"Yes, Ma'am." She quietly walked up the stairs and within a couple of minutes Charles Hancock came down. He was slim and tall for an eleven-year-old, with strong, even features and braces on his teeth.

"Charles, this is Samuel Hamilton. He wants to ask you some questions about Phillip and Bruce. He's a reporter and he's also helping the police investigate the crimes."

"I thought they already caught the man who killed them. That's what Tony told us."

"I'm afraid not. He'll explain that to you, son.

"Would you prefer that I not be present, Mr. Hamilton? I know that children can be circumspect when parents are around."

"If you don't mind, Mrs. Hancock. You're right. Kids are more reserved with their parents around. Just let us talk for a few minutes. If we run into any problems, Charles will call you, I'm sure."

Mrs. Hancock left the room with her glass of sherry, and Samuel turned to the boy. "I'm sure these deaths have been painful to the boys in your class. I'm sorry that I have to bring back unpleasant memories, but the truth is that the kidnapping and murder cases haven't been solved. The man Tony's father accuses just wasn't involved. So here we are, Charles. Are you willing to help me?"

Charles gave a wan smile. "If I can, Mr. Hamilton. I don't know very much. I wasn't close to either of them."

"I was told by someone that you called Phillip a queer."

Charles blushed. "Yes," he stammered. "I did, but it was kind of a joke. He was kissing up to Marcus Johns, the owner of the summer camp. After that, everyone who heard me say it joined in and carried on with the joke."

Samuel looked up from his notebook in surprise. "Who is Marcus Johns? I've heard that name before."

"He owns a summer camp where a lot of boys go for athletics."

"You mean boys from Towne School, including Phillip and Bruce, right?"

"Yes, but not just from Towne School."

"Where's the camp that he takes you?"

"No, no. He picks us up in a VW bus and takes us to city parks, like Golden Gate."

Samuel looked up slowly, and he squinted at the boy. He remembered looking at Johns' powder blue VW bus when he was trying to find Alain's kidnapper. "What a coincidence!" he thought.

"Do you know Diego Altamira?"

"Diego Altamira?" responded Charles, a bit surprised that Samuel knew his name. "I think there was boy by that name in the group last summer."

"From the Marina?"

"Yeah, that's him. He lives on Chestnut," said Charles, still a bit surprised.

"Can you tell me how to get hold of Marcus?" Samuel asked in as calm a voice as he could muster.

"Ah, I have a flier upstairs for this summer. It came last week."

"Can I get a copy of that?" asked Samuel.

"Sure, I'm not going this summer because we're going to

Italy. You can have it."

"Did any of the boys ever have any trouble with Mr. Johns while you were at summer camp?"

"No. I have been with his summer camp for three years, and I never heard any complaints from anyone."

"What about from Phillip or his friend Bruce?"

"Nope, none that I know of."

Samuel asked Charles to go upstairs and get the flier. He did and came downstairs and handed it to Samuel.

"Thanks for your help, Charles. Do you mind if I call you if I have any more questions?" he said in a rushed manner.

"No problem. But remember, I'm going to Europe."

"Yes, I know that. When do you leave?"

"In three weeks."

"I'll just have to work fast if I need your help. Can you call your mom? I want to thank her too."

Charles called his mother, who came to the head of the stairs but hesitated there, looking as if she'd had enough of a shock for one day. When Samuel saw that she wasn't coming down, he said, "Thank you very much, Mrs. Hancock. Your son's been a big help."

She waved in an off-handed way, and he walked out the door and down the stairs of the mansion to the street.

As soon as he hit the pavement, he checked his notebook and saw that the address that Charles had given him for Johns was the same one he had visited near the beach. He walked rapidly and finally began to run as fast as he could to the nearest phone booth. He found one at a gas station at California and Arguello streets. From there he called Bernardi and told him what he had just found out and made him promise not to leave his office before he got there. Samuel then decided to forgo his cheapskate practice of taking the bus and hailed a cab. He made it to Bryant Street in twenty minutes instead of the usual hour it would have taken.

* * *

Not bothering to wait for the elevator, Samuel ran up four flights of stairs, past the Homicide receptionist, and directly into Bernardi's office, where he found the lieutenant on the phone asking if there was a rap sheet on Marcus Johns.

"We need to know where this young man went to school and get his records," said Samuel, out of breath.

"We're already on that. He's goes to City College of San Francisco."

"Can you loan me a patrolman who can take me and my photographer to his house near the beach in the next hour or so."

"What for?"

"Remember he owns a VW bus, and we ignored it because it wasn't yellow. I want to see what kind of tires it has on it and get an impression of them, just in case he tries to get rid of the vehicle."

With Bernardi's permission and the address in hand, Samuel called Marcel. He told the photographer that he and a patrolman were going to pick him up in the next few minutes to go out and take some photos.

"I'm just trying to get something that will stick. Right now we don't have shit."

"Well, we do have shit. We just don't know who it belongs to," said Bernardi, laughing. Looking out the window at the congested freeway, he added, "This could be a wild goose chase, so don't go overboard trying to get evidence that we won't be able to use because you violated this young man's rights."

This left Samuel with the impression that Bernardi wasn't impressed with the find. "Let's see what comes up. If you get anything at all, I'll bring him in for questioning."

* * *

Samuel, the patrolman, and Marcel went out to the Avenues in the Sunset District near Ocean Beach. They approached a faded blue Volkswagen bus. It had letters on the side that read, "Johns' Summer Camp" and the telephone number that Samuel had seen on the flier.

He asked the patrolman to park down the street away from Johns' house. Marcel started taking photos while there was still enough light to do so without using a flash. He and Samuel got next to the bus, and Marcel took close-up photos of the tire treads. Samuel took a piece of paper out of his notebook and traced all four tire treads as Marcel photographed him doing it, so he would have photos and an outline. That way, Mac could compare them to the casts he had made at the crime scene. Just as he was finishing his tracing a nice-looking young man engaged them. He was of medium height and weight with brown hair cut short, and a very pleasant but strange smile.

"You fellows need some help?" he asked, almost too eagerly.

Samuel immediately recognized Johns. "We're just looking around," he said, smiling. "We were just out at the beach taking some photos of the sea lions, and we're on our way back to my office to write an article about them," he said, trying to give an excuse for the presence of the photographer.

Johns ignored the comments, chatted pleasantly with them for a couple of minutes, and left.

All three of them watched him enter his home. Samuel grimaced because he had little doubt that Johns recognized him, too. He shook his head. "I hope he didn't see us fiddling with his car. Now I feel lucky we got the photos and the tracings, I wouldn't put it past the suspect to change the tires before the police can get his car impounded.

"Thank goodness the bus was on public property. Imagine our problems if it was in his garage, and he caught us in there?"

Marcel laughed. "You're a lucky bastard, Samuel. You always come out on top."

Samuel didn't feel so lucky. He knew that Johns parked his bus on the street, and he kicked himself in the butt for not seeing the connection before Charles mentioned him as the owner of the Summer Camp. "He knows who I am. Let's get out of here. We have to move fast."

They returned rapidly to Bryant Street. Samuel turned over the tracings to Mac, who was waiting for them. Samuel went upstairs to talk with Bernardi. "We'd better hurry and get that car impounded. He recognized me from our last trip to his house," and related what happened at the scene.

"What does Mac say about the tire treads? Do they match?"

"He said he had to wait until tomorrow when he sees Marcel's photos. I tried to get him to give us an opinion, just based on the tracings I made, but he said he wanted to wait."

"We should have most of Johns' records by tomorrow, including his college, high school, and mental health records, if he has any. In the meantime, do you have a phone number for your shrink, Doctor Vishinski? If you do, will you call him and see if we can talk to him around ten tomorrow?"

"I'm sure he'll want to help," said Samuel, "but I don't think we should wait until tomorrow. I think you should bring Johns in now and impound his bus. Remember what Dr. Vishinski said. This guy, if it's him, is dangerous, and he's capable of pulling off a lot of tricks, especially since he already saw us snooping around. The shrink will just repeat what he told me, that we have to look for specific things. Shitting at the scene of the crime is only one of them. Starting fires and being cruel to animals and causing trouble in school are also in the mix."

"Let me repeat my concern. I'm not sure you're on the right track. I remember Mr. Johns. And I'm not convinced that that young man we saw is our suspect. We know he's hanging around young kids. Do you really think he could hide a serious mental illness from his victims until he got them in his clutches? We need proof if we're going to go after him," warned Bernardi.

"My intuition tells me that it's him, and we're just wasting time," said Samuel, annoyed and frustrated at Bernardi's reluctance to act. He looked over and saw him standing behind his desk with his fists clenched and his arms folded. "Hell, Samuel, I'll say it again, we need evidence, not intuition."

Samuel felt they would pay a huge price for it.

* * *

The next day, Samuel and Bernardi spent an hour on the phone with Dr. Vishinski. After their conversation, Bernardi agreed that Johns should be brought in for questioning, and that his bus should be impounded and inspected until the interrogation was completed.

A squad car with two officers and a tow truck went to Johns' address and arrested him in order to bring him downtown for questioning, but his bus was nowhere to be found. He claimed it had been stolen, and that he'd reported it. Samuel was in his office with Bernardi when he heard the news. "Goddammit, Bernardi, I told you this might happen. We should have acted last night when I got back from his house." Samuel stormed out of Bernardi's office and went downstairs to the basement café to have a cup of coffee and calm himself down.

* * *

Seated at the interrogation table facing the two-way mirror was Marcus Johns, wearing a City College sweatshirt and blue jeans that matched his collegiate looks.

Samuel, watching from his usual perch behind the mirror,

had already observed Johns' quick wit. This was reaffirmed by the college records that noted his IQ was 150. But he was still perplexed by the strange smile. Across from Johns was Assistant Deputy District Attorney Dante Capuro, Bruno Bernardi, the head of homicide, Sergeant Ivan Patruski, the head of kidnapping, and a plainclothesman also from homicide. There was also a tape recorder on the table with microphones directly in front of Johns and Bernardi.

Samuel was surprised that Johns showed up by himself, but he had been warned by Dr. Vishinski that one of the characteristics he could expect to see was a feeling of superiority and the belief that he could talk his way out of all attacks against him, written or verbal. Bernardi started the interrogation. "Mr. Johns, do you understand that I'm putting you under oath and that you are being asked to tell the truth, the whole truth and nothing but the truth, so help you God?"

"Yes, sir, I understand, and I swear I will."

"Okay, first give me your name."

"My name is Marcus Johns. You already know my address because your officers picked me up there this morning." He smiled.

"Tell me what you do for a living?"

"I am a student at City College of San Francisco, studying physics and mathematics, and I'm working my way through school."

"I have your records here, and I see that you are a straight A student. Looks like you're a pretty smart fellow?"

"I do my best, Mr. Bernardi. It's not easy working and going to school."

"I imagine it's not, and I imagine you don't have much free time, even to grab a bite to eat."

"You're right about that."

"So where do you eat?"

"To be honest with you, Lieutenant, most of the time I

grab a hot dog at a Doggie Diner. They're cheap and filling and pretty darn good."

"I can vouch for them. I've had a few myself," said Bernardi, and everyone laughed.

Samuel remembered the Polish sausage or hot dog fragments that were found in the human excrement, and wrote a note in his notebook. "This guy is definitely a smooth son of a bitch. It would really be awful if he talks his way out of this."

"Let's get back to school for a moment. Have you ever been disciplined for any reason?"

"At any time, in all the years I've been at school?"

"Yes, that's what I'm asking."

"I had my hands smacked with a ruler by the principal for horsing around now and then, when I was in grade school, but nothing else comes to mind."

"You've never been punished at school for starting fires in the boy's and girl's bathrooms on the same day?"

Johns raised his eyebrows and looked shocked. "Are you kidding? Not me."

"Or even made to tour the fire department with your parents for trying to set your parents' house on fire?" asked Bernardi, looking down as if he were reading from documents right in front of him.

Johns shook his head nonchalantly and stared directly at Bernardi with an expression on his face that was an attempt to assure the Lieutenant that he was being confused with someone else.

"Were you ever visited by the Humane Society and asked to explain why you were drowning stray cats?"

"No, sir. I love animals. As a matter of fact, I have two cats."

"I bet," thought Samuel.

"Let's talk about your summer camp for young boys. How did you get started with that?"

"I used to babysit for a family in Pacific Heights, the Jacksons. Mrs. Jackson asked me if I would be interested in taking some boys out for exercise and game playing during the summer months. She told me she could get some other boys besides her two sons to participate if I was interested. I said, of course I was, and that's how I got started."

"Did you have to have a city license in order to do that?"

"It never came up, so I didn't honestly know it was needed. I don't have a city license, if that's what you're asking."

"Do you have a place where the boys are brought for this summer camp of yours?"

"No. I bought a Volkswagen bus and had my name and phone number painted on the side of it. I pick up the boys at their homes and take them to parks and museums in the city."

"How many boys are in your summer camp?"

"I limit it to seven each summer. I have a waiting list, and if a boy goes on vacation, I call another one's parents and make room for him."

"Where is that bus now?"

"It was stolen last night," he said, looking toward Bernardi calmly.

"I see that," said Bernardi, looking at a another piece of paper. "This report says you called the police at 11:30 P.M. last night. That's pretty late to notice it had disappeared, don't you think?"

Samuel was beside himself behind the mirror. Why in hell didn't Bernardi listen to me? We would really have this bastard if we had that vehicle. He pounded his fists together and was pacing the small enclosure in utter frustration.

"I heard some noise outside my house, and I recognized the sound of the engine running. When I heard it and realized it was my bus, I rushed outside and saw it going down the street rapidly. I ran back inside and called the police."

"Have you changed the tires on that bus in the last year?"

"No, sir. They are in good shape. I had them checked at Sears where I bought them just last month. I am getting ready for this year's summer camp."

"Did anyone besides you have a key to that bus?"

"No one but me."

Samuel felt the case slipping away. Johns' presentation was good, and the evidence was lacking.

"Do you own a firearm?"

Johns opened his eyes wide and had a surprised look on his face. "You mean a gun?"

"Yes. A pistol?"

"No, sir. Don't know the first thing about them."

"Do you know what a .38 is?"

"No, sir."

"Will you write a few sentences on this pad of paper for me?" Bernardi handed a blank yellow legal pad to him.

"What do you want me to write?"

"Oh, anything. Try, 'How now brown cow.' Just write it several times."

Although Samuel couldn't see what Bernardi had in his hands because his back was to him, he assumed it was one or both of the ransom notes that the killer had presumably written after the first two killings.

When Johns finished writing, he sat back and folded his arms in front of him with a self-satisfied look. A police officer knocked and entered the room and handed Bernardi a sheaf of papers that looked like it contained a police report. Bernardi read it and passed it to the other authorities in the room. After seeing and reading it, they all smiled. Johns just stared straight ahead avoiding eye contact.

"Here's our problem, Mr. Johns. There have been three murders in this city in the last few months, and all three boys were in your summer camp. You knew that, didn't you?"

"They were all fine boys, too."

"Did you ever meet any of these boys alone for any reason?"

"The only reason I would be alone with any of them would be if they were the first one I picked up or the last one I dropped off."

"But you never just took them out alone?"

"No, sir."

"Or told them to meet you at the market on California Street."

"No, sir."

"Or had sex with any of them?"

"What? Are you kidding?"

"And you never shot any of them in the head with a .38 pistol that you owned?"

"What kind of a question is that? Of course not!"

"Or one that you borrowed from someone else?"

"No, sir."

"And you didn't defecate in the alleyway South of Market after you killed each of them?"

Now Johns looked tense, and his smile was gone. His eyes almost closed, and they looked to Samuel like the slits of two snake eyes. "No! Look it, I've been here for a long time now, and I've answered all your questions. I think it's about time I left now." He started to get up and rubbed his hands together as if he were trying to wipe off the sweat.

The plainclothes police officer stood up, walked over, and put his hands on Johns' shoulders. "You're not going anywhere, Mr. Johns," said Bernardi.

"The report I just received was that your bus was recovered this morning from Lake Merced, and in it was a .38 pistol with what may be your fingerprints on it and a couple of boxes of .38 caliber bullets. In addition, ballistics has already confirmed that bullets fired from that gun killed all three boys."

"That's it, we got him," laughed Samuel, and he jumped up and down with a big smile on his face. He was happy.

"My bus?" he said, startled.

"Yes, and the truth is, Mr. Johns, we have proof that the tires on your bus went through one of the piles of excrement that you left at the scene where you murdered the boys that you had sex with. We have the photos of your tires. We have tracings of them, and now we have the actual tires themselves.

"Marcus Johns, you're under arrest for the murders of Phillip Atkinson, Bruce Axelrod, and Diego Altamira. Cuff him and get him out of here," said Bernardi. "He makes me sick."

Johns now looked bewildered and red-faced. He tried to say something, but the words wouldn't come out. Instead, he looked at the floor and tried to loosen the handcuffs that were holding his hands behind his back. "You've got the wrong guy," he stammered. "I'm innocent. I'm just a struggling college student."

Samuel, behind the mirror, had a broad and relieved smile on his face. He couldn't believe it was over. Just a few days ago he thought it was going nowhere. After they carted Johns away, he went into the interrogation room. Patruski was still sitting in his seat looking dumbfounded. "I really thought that the Frenchman did it. How could I be so wrong?" he said, looking worn out.

"You need a couple of days off, Sergeant," said Bernardi.

Samuel continued smiling. "Dr. Vishinski nailed the personality type, didn't he?"

"Johns had a lot of people fooled," said Bernardi, "including me. I'm grateful you convinced me to talk to your shrink, Samuel. Otherwise that bastard would still be walking around planning his next murder."

"What a relief. Now I have to rush to my office and write my story for a late edition of this afternoon's paper before anyone else gets their hands on my story, and I have to tell Emma that the killer has been caught. Will I see you at Camelot this evening, Bruno?"

"Why not? I'll have a drink to the end of this nightmare."

Samuel went to his office a happy and, at the same time, a sad man. He was thinking of the boys who had lost their lives and about the creep that took them. He also thought about his fears that Alain might have been among them and his relief in finding the young boy safe. And finally there was the help of his favorite dog, Excalibur. Late in the afternoon, his story was released in an extra edition of the afternoon paper. The headline blared:

ALLEGED KILLER OF THREE BOYS CAUGHT.
BRILLIANT POLICE WORK NAILS PSYCHOPATH.

The edition sold out in an hour and a half.

* * *

That evening Samuel and Bernardi were sitting around the Round Table with Melba. She was having her usual beer and smoking a Lucky Strike. Bernardi was drinking red wine, and Samuel was sipping scotch over the rocks. Excalibur was by his side chewing on the treat Samuel had just given him.

Melba looked good in her new black dress with white polka dots and had just been to the hairdresser to get her hair tinted blue. "Blanche told me she would be here in a half hour and said not to leave before she got here."

Samuel smiled. "She told me the same thing. We're going to Doro's for dinner tonight. I already made reservations. I invited Emma and Reyna to join us."

"How did you pull this one off, Samuel?" she asked.

"It comes down to luck. The kidnapping of Alain got me off the track. It was so important to me to find him that I stopped looking for the killer [illegible]ng it might be Levantine.

After we found Maurice and learned why he took Alain and were able to bring Alain back home, we had to fight off Patruski who wanted to hang the kidnapping and all the murders on Levantine. That got us even further away from finding the real killer."

"What was the key?" asked Melba as she took a long drag on her cigarette.

"The real key was when Bernardi and I went out to Johns' house looking for the yellow VW bus that was used to kidnap Alain. Since Johns' was blue, I didn't make the connection. But when I learned from the Hancock boy that Marcus Johns had a summer camp, it all started to fall into place because I remembered he owned a blue VW bus."

Bernardi didn't say anything because he'd lagged behind on the investigation. He tipped his glass to Samuel for putting it all together.

Samuel also explained that Levantine would now plead guilty to the kidnapping charge. He would spend some years in the state penitentiary and then be deported.

Just then, Blanche walked in dressed in white with her blond hair pulled back in a ponytail. She kissed her mother and then Samuel and sat down next to him in the chair he'd saved for her. "You're a hero again, Samuel. Tell me all about it."

"I'll tell you at dinner," he said with a huge smile on his face. "You're going to meet Emma, Reyna, and Alain."

"Who's Reyna?"

"She's the grandmother. We have to leave because we have a reservation in North Beach at Doro's."

Everyone got up, and Samuel and Blanche were ready to leave. Samuel gave another treat to Excalibur and again thanked Melba for loaning him the dog. "You know that he inspired Snoop, the police dog, to help find Alain. He was a real star, just as he was in the case of the Chinese Jars."